A
PARTING
GIFT

BEN ERICKSON

A
PARTING
GIFT

Published in Large Print by arrangement with Warner Books, Inc. in the United States and Canada.

Wheeler Large Print Book Series.

Set in 16 pt Plantin.

Grateful acknowledgment is given for permission to reprint the following:
Excerpt reprinted with permission of Scribner, a Division of Simon & Schuster, from *The Old Man and the Sea* by Ernest Hemingway. Copyright 1952 by Ernest Hemingway. Copyright renewed © 1980 by Mary Hemingway.
Excerpt from a poem by T'ao Ch'ien from *A Hundred and Seventy Chinese Poems* translated by Arthur Waley. Copyright 1919 by Alfred A. Knopf, Inc.
Excerpt from *A River Runs Through It* by Norman Maclean reprinted with permission of The University of Chicago Press. Copyright © 1976 by The University of Chicago.
Valedictorian speech reprinted by permission of William E. Erickson. Copyright 1996 by William E. Erickson.
Excerpt by Hermann Hesse, from *Siddhartha* (translated by Hilda Rosner). Copyright © 1951 by New Directions Publishing Corp. Reprinted by permission of New Directions Publishing Corp.
Excerpt from *The Sirens of Titan* by Kurt Vonnegut, Jr., Delacorte Press, a division of Bantam Doubleday Dell. Copyright © 1959 by Kurt Vonnegut, Jr.

Library of Congress Cataloging-in-Publication Data

Erickson, Ben.
    A parting gift / Ben Erickson.
        p. (large print) cm.(Wheeler large print book series)
    ISBN 1-56895-932-X (hardcover)
    1. Reminiscing in old age—Fiction. 2. Male friendship—Fiction.
3. Mobile (Ala.)—Fiction. 4. Teenage boys—Fiction. 5. Aged men—
Fiction. 6. Large type books. I. Title.

[PS3555.R4267 P37   2000b]
813'.54—dc21   00-043670
                                                              CIP

To my eldest son,

Bill

Acknowledgments

It has been said that no man is an island, and this is true of books as well. You would not be reading this book today if it were not for some very special people:

To my wife, deLancey, who believed in this book from the beginning and encouraged me to keep going.

To my agent, Theresa Park, for taking the time to read an unpublished writer's work and seeing beyond the rough edges.

To my editor, Jamie Raab, who gently nudged me in the right direction, and everyone else at Warner Books for making dreams come true.

To my son Bill, for providing the inspiration for writing this book.

To my son Ben, for helping me with the sometimes magical and often mysterious workings of computers.

To all the writers who have made my life richer than it was before.

Chapter 1

Occupational Hazard

The beat-up old Volkswagen, radio blaring, puttered up the long drive to the house. Ancient live oaks lined the drive and formed a living arch over it. The house sat far off the road, and it wasn't until rounding the last bend that the bay came into view.

The house was unpainted and covered in battered clapboard siding that had weathered to a silvery gray. On the tree-shaded back, the combination of little sunlight and high humidity had provided a fertile place for mold and mildew to grow. It has been said that you can watch wood decompose before your very eyes in the sweltering southern climate, and—like many things in the South—it was almost true.

Still, the house had been built when things were made to last. When time was measured more by the sun and the passing of the seasons than the ticking of a clock. Only the best virgin cypress was used, cut from trees found in a swamp less than a mile from the house itself. The hand-hewed mortise-and-tenon construction had marked the turning of a century and two world wars with little notice. It had even survived the frequent hurricanes that hit Mobile Bay, when the only warning of an approaching storm was the movement of animals or the stiffening of joints. With the passing of the years, the house had settled down to fit in with the curve of the bay and the slope of the hill until it seemed as if it had been standing there forever.

The tires crunched on the loose clamshells as the car rounded the last bend in the drive. On the radio, Jimi Hendrix blasted out at full tilt—the thin sheet metal resonating with the sound. The VW skidded to a stop next to a massive Buick, and its motor coughed, sputtered, and finally died. As the rust-pitted driver's door swung open with a reluctant squeal, a boy of seventeen stepped out, pushing his sun-streaked hair back behind his ears to keep it from falling across his face. This, coupled with the surfboard rack bolted to the roof of his car, was a sure indicator that he spent as much time as possible at the beach twenty miles to the south.

Humming softly to the song that was still playing in his head, he flipped the front seat forward, reached into the back, and took out the last of what had once been a substantial stack of foam food containers. Leaving the car door hanging open, he walked quickly across the drive to the house. He took the steps two at a time and knocked out the rhythm to the song on the back door, his head bobbing slightly to an imaginary drummer.

No answer.

He knocked again, harder.

Nothing.

Pulling on the door, he found it locked and loped back down the steps and around to the bay side of the house. He scanned the yard for the old man's stooped back or broad-brimmed hat, then trudged up the front steps and across the porch and knocked again.

Silence.

This time the knob turned easily in his hand, and he opened the door just enough to stick his head inside.

"Mr. Davis?" he called loudly. "It's me, Josh Bell. I've got your dinner."

The house remained quiet.

He opened the door the rest of the way and walked down the entry hall to the kitchen, dropping the container on the breakfast table. His job complete, he retraced his steps to the front door, then paused as he started to close it behind him. An imperceptible shudder ran through him as he thought of Mrs. Miller last year. He had been the first to find her— cold and stiff as a board, still lying in her bed. An occupational hazard, he guessed, kind of like that old movie *Ten Little Indians*. Except there were twelve—well, now eleven— he delivered meals to, and they weren't being stalked by a psychotic killer, just the relentless specter of death. Fearing the worst, he turned with a sigh and reentered the house, walking down the hall toward the two bedrooms.

"Mr. Davis?" he said, knocking lightly on one of the closed doors.

There was no answer, so he opened it and looked inside. The room was furnished with twin beds that were neatly made, but otherwise it appeared bare and unused.

He crossed the hall and knocked on the other door. At his touch, it creaked slowly inward on its hinges. An antique double bed dominated the room, its dark wood in sharp contrast with the stark white walls. Books were piled on the bedside table, and a shirt was draped over a chair in the corner. The bed was neatly made, though he saw the toe of a slipper protruding from beneath the dust ruffle. But for all these signs of life, it too was empty.

He tried the bathroom at the end of the hall.

Nothing.

"Mr. Davis?" he called again, still hoping for a response.

He passed the narrow staircase in the entry hall and started up it, then decided that the old man probably wouldn't attempt to scale the steep steps at his age. He continued across the hall to the living room that overlooked the bay, but there was no sign of life there, either.

That left only the den off the kitchen. Backtracking, he walked through the kitchen and slowly pushed open the door to the den. A reading lamp was on, but the aged wood paneling seemed to absorb the light as soon as it left the bulb, and the shade from the oaks outside allowed little of the late afternoon sun to penetrate. He squinted in the dim light as he looked around the room. Except for the fireplace, almost all of the walls were lined with bookcases.

Only then did he notice the shape lying in the tilted-back recliner.

A wrinkled hand dangled toward a book, which lay open on the floor beside the still figure. The other hand was folded limply across his chest. The old man's head was thrown back and his eyes were closed, but his mouth hung slightly open.

Except for the ticking of the clock on the mantel shelf, the room was shrouded in silence. Josh walked slowly over to where the body lay and hesitantly reached out to touch it, checking to see if it was cold yet. He swallowed hard as his fingers neared the splotched skin, forcing them to make contact. There was a jerk, as if electricity had run through the inert frame, and the old man's eyes flew open. Josh stumbled backward with a start, hitting his head hard on a corner of the mantel.

"What are you doing, boy!" Mr. Davis said gruffly, sitting up in his chair.

"I—I—" Josh stammered.

"You what."

"I thought you—"

"Hasn't anyone ever taught you to knock?" the old man interrupted.

"I did, but I—"

"As I see it, your job is to leave my supper on the kitchen table, not go snooping around my house."

"It's just that I thought—I mean—Mrs. Miller—I was the one who—" Josh faltered.

"Spit it out, son. You act like you've seen a ghost."

"I have—I mean—it's just that you didn't answer the door, and I thought that you might be...you know..." The old man sat there with a puzzled expression on his face, so Josh was left with no choice. "Dead," he said, finishing the sentence.

The room was silent as his words sank slowly to the floor. Mr. Davis stared at the boy for a minute, then he relaxed and smiled.

"Well, as you can plainly see, I'm not," he said. "Not yet, at least. I was reading, and I must have dozed off."

"I—I'll be going then...that is, if you're okay and everything," Josh said, rubbing his head and backing slowly toward the door.

"I'm fine, son, I assure you," he replied, starting to get up.

"Well, I left your dinner on the kitchen table...in the kitchen, that is."

Josh turned to bolt from the room and instead ran into a bookcase beside the door. There was a loud crash, and he suddenly found himself on the floor, covered in a cascade of falling books. He started to climb to his feet, but they gave way beneath him. From a great distance he could hear the voice of the old man calling him.

"Boy?...Josh?"

He felt as if he were at the bottom of a well and the circle of light at the top seemed miles away. Gradually he floated up or the light seemed to settle down. Mr. Davis leaned over and helped him to a sitting position as Steinbeck and Twain poured off him like water.

"I'm okay," Josh muttered sheepishly as he sat there on the floor, gathering himself.

"I think you had better rest a minute until you feel better," Mr. Davis said. "You've had a nasty shock, and that bump on your head could use some tending to."

He helped Josh to the kitchen table and fixed an ice pack for his head.

"How about some iced tea?" he inquired, trying to take the boy's mind off what had happened.

"I'm fine, really," Josh said, putting the ice pack on the table and starting to get up. "I should be going now."

The old man put a hand on his shoulder. "No, sit. I insist."

Josh gave in and slumped back into the chair. Mr. Davis looked over at the boy as he opened the refrigerator. "That ice isn't going to do any good if you don't use it," he said sternly.

Josh closed his eyes and returned the ice pack to his head. Mr. Davis put two glasses on the table in front of them and pulled up a chair. Josh took a sip and looked down at the table, pretending to examine his glass.

The old man stared at his lowered head for a minute. "What grade are you in, son?" he finally asked.

Josh shifted the ice pack to his other hand. "I'm a senior," he said.

"Well, that makes two of us," Mr. Davis quipped, and noticed the boy's faint smile in response. "At least that's what they like to call us nowadays. Any idea what you'll do after graduation?" he asked.

"I'm not sure yet," Josh answered, still avoiding the old man's gaze. "I'd like to go to college if I get a scholarship. If not, I guess I'll try to find a job around here."

He looked at the spot of blood on the ice pack, then returned it to the growing lump.

"How are your grades?"

"Pretty good," he said tentatively, taking another sip of tea.

"Do you like school?" Mr. Davis asked after another long pause.

Josh thought for a minute. "I guess so. I mean, you're not really supposed to like it, are you?"

The old man chuckled. "No, I guess not. Do you read much, Josh?"

"A little. We're reading some novels in English this year."

"Stuffy old classics, I'll bet."

"Mostly," Josh said. "*The Scarlet Letter, Wuthering Heights*, things like that."

"Ever go to the library and check out a book just for fun?" Mr. Davis pressed.

"Sometimes," he answered, wondering where all this was leading.

"Anything that you really liked? That you couldn't put down?"

The boy glanced up at him. "There was a book of short stories by Jimmy Buffett—you know, the singer."

"What was it that you liked about it?"

"I'm not sure," Josh said. "I guess that it was about people who were kind of different."

"What do you mean, different?"

"Well..." He thought for a minute. "It was like everything they did or said was bigger and brighter than the way things really are," he said, looking directly at the old man for the first time.

"Go on."

Josh's brow furrowed. "And even though some of the stories took place right around here," he said, searching for the right words, "it really wasn't like anywhere I've ever been before."

He looked at the older man, a little surprised by his own insights. Mr. Davis nodded and smiled.

"That's what books do best," he said.

"What?" Josh asked.

"They create their own world. A world you care about and love, but could never visit in real life. Books can pluck you out of your everyday experiences and carry you somewhere far away."

Josh considered this. "I think I know what you mean," he said. "I feel like I knew those characters. It was like I've lived with them always, but they're not even close to being like anybody that I really know."

Mr. Davis got up and disappeared into the den. He returned with the book he had been reading earlier and put it on the table in front of him.

"Do you know who Ernest Hemingway is?" he said, sitting down again.

"Sure, a writer. But he's dead, isn't he?"

"Yes, but his books are still with us, so in

a sense he'll never die. Not as long as there are people who read what he has written. That's one of the beauties of writing, Josh. It's like adding a drop to the sea of man's knowledge and experiences." He looked out the window at the branches framed against the deepening sky.

"Have you ever read this?" Mr. Davis asked, pushing the thin book across the table to him.

Josh picked it up and flipped through it. The yellowing pages had been thumbed through many times over the years. He shook his head.

"Well, take it home and give it a try. Let me know what you think."

"Sure," he said as he got up to leave.

Dusk had fallen and the temperature was starting to drop when Josh left the house and walked over to his car. As he slipped the book into the pocket of his jacket, he looked back through the window at the old man sitting alone at the kitchen table.

It was well after dark when Josh pulled into the driveway of the small house that he had painted himself last summer. He cut the engine and sat for a moment, looking down the row of similar houses in the faint glow of the streetlights. As he got out, he noticed for the first time that the bulbs his mother had planted in the flower bed were beginning to come up.

It had been six years since the divorce and

over a year since he had last seen his father. He was an only child, and life hadn't been easy since the breakup. His mother worked the early shift at the twenty-four-hour discount store that had opened in town last year, then somehow found time to fix the twelve—now eleven—meals for the elderly that he delivered after school. The extra income from the "meal on wheels" business helped make ends meet, and when his father remembered to send the child support check, things went smoothly. Things rarely went smoothly.

Josh opened the kitchen door to find his mother washing dishes at the sink. She glanced in his direction, reproaching him silently. "Sorry I'm late," he said quickly. "Mr. Davis kept me awhile."

"Next time call," she said, turning off the water. "You know how I worry about you being on the road in that old car at night."

"I will," he said contritely, giving her a peck on the cheek as she dried her hands on a dishtowel. "It's a long story."

She took their still warm plates out of the oven, and they sat down to eat. Josh related the events of the afternoon and told her about his conversation with the old man.

"Well, he's always seemed nice," she said. "And I guess he's been lonely since his wife died. That house has been in his family for generations, but they had only moved back here a few years when it happened. He's become almost a hermit since then."

She put down her fork and folded her hands,

staring at their diffused reflections in the kitchen window. Josh looked at her and noticed for the first time how tired and thin she had become.

"Now that you mention it, I don't think I've ever seen him in town," he said to keep the conversation going.

She glanced at him and picked up her fork again.

"I see him from time to time," she said. "He comes in to pick up supplies and go to the library. But he always seems to look right through you." She picked at her food. "He only shops at Hinson's Grocery and the old hardware store next door. I heard him say that the new discount store is a gift from the devil, and sometimes I feel like he's right. I don't know what he'll do if Hinson's goes out of business, and how they stay *in* business, I'll never know."

"He goes to the library a lot, huh?" Josh asked as he finished his last bite and put down his fork.

"He's a regular. When I filled in there last year, he came in every week and always left with a stack of books. Not much of a talker, though. Friendly, but he seems uncomfortable making small talk."

"Well, he talked a lot to me today."

"Maybe that's because he had something to say," she said, getting up from the table.

Josh cleared the dishes before he started on his homework while his mother went in the other room to watch television. He was still working when she came in and kissed him good night, gently fingering the lump on his forehead.

"Sleep tight," she said as she closed the door to her room.

"You too," he answered, a little too late.

Later, as he was hanging up his coat, the book Mr. Davis had given him fell out of the pocket. He picked it up and rubbed his fingers over the waterstained cover, then climbed into bed and turned on the lamp. As he opened it, he could smell the musty odor of the old man's house so close to the bay. Turning to the first page, he began to read:

He was an old man who fished alone in a skiff in the Gulf Stream and he had gone eighty-four days now without taking a fish. In the first forty days a boy had been with him. But after forty days without a fish the boy's parents had told him that the old man was now definitely and finally *salao*, which is the worst form of unlucky, and the boy had gone at their orders in another boat which caught three good fish the first week. It made the boy sad to see the old man come in each day with his skiff empty and he always went down to help him carry either the coiled lines or the gaff and harpoon and the sail that was furled around the mast. The sail was patched with flour sacks and, furled, it looked like the flag of permanent defeat.

Chapter 2

Storm Damage

A front pushed through during the night, bringing a line of thunderstorms with it that rumbled their way across the bay. When Josh drove up the drive to Mr. Davis's house the next afternoon, he stopped to move a limb blocking the road that had snapped off one of the oaks in the storm. As he pulled, there was a flash of color and a flutter of wings, and a small bedraggled bird freed itself from underneath. It sat on the clamshells, ruffling its blue feathers, but didn't fly away.

Josh dragged the limb off the road and walked back to his car, then noticed the bird still sitting there in front of him. "Shoo," he said, waving his arms, but it didn't budge. He walked over to it, but the bird held its ground, so he reached down to pick it up. It avoided his grasp and attempted to fly, only to flop helplessly on the grass a few feet away. As the bird regained its feet, Josh noticed that one wing protruded at an awkward angle.

He approached it slowly this time. "Don't be scared," he said in a soothing voice. "I'm not going to hurt you."

Kneeling next to it, he held out his hands slowly. The bird drew back and opened its beak in defense but didn't try to fly this time.

"Easy now," he said softly. "There's nothing to be afraid of."

Josh reached out and cupped the bird in his outstretched hands. It struggled briefly, then seemed to relax. He held it up to eye level and looked at it. The bird cocked its head and eyed him suspiciously.

"See, I told you I wouldn't hurt you," he said as he rubbed it gently.

The bird made a sound deep in its throat and closed its eyes, exhausted. Josh could feel the rapid beating of its heart beneath his fingers as he smoothed the iridescent feathers.

He walked back to the car and got in. Holding the bird against his chest with one hand, he started up the VW and put it in gear with the other. Leaving the car door open, he coasted slowly the rest of the way up the drive, then cut the engine. After getting out carefully, he walked up to the house with the bird still nestled against him.

Mr. Davis had been watching through his kitchen window as he did the dishes, and he was waiting for Josh at the door when he walked up.

"What have you got there?" he asked.

"I found it in the driveway," the boy said, opening his hands a little so the old man could see. "I think it has a broken wing."

"A bluebird," the old man observed. "They're pretty hard to find around here these days. I nailed some boxes up on the trees last year for them to nest in, but I guess this one didn't get in out of the storm."

"What can we do?"

"It's usually better to let nature take care of its own," Mr. Davis said, rubbing his chin.

Josh looked down at the small ball of feathers in his hands. "But you said they were rare," he countered. "Maybe we could just keep it until it's better, then let it go."

"What do you mean 'we,'" Mr. Davis said with a smile.

"Well...I'll keep it, then," the boy said, seeming suddenly very sure of himself.

"It's not that simple," the old man said. "Wild things often don't do well in captivity. And if it does survive, you'll have to take care of it: feed it, change the paper in the bottom of the cage—"

"No problem," Josh replied.

Mr. Davis looked at the boy and saw the determination in his eyes.

"Well, bring it in and let's take a look," he said.

"Thanks," Josh said, smiling.

Josh held the bird on the kitchen table while Mr. Davis examined it. He carefully stretched out the injured wing, and the bird let out a series of high-pitched peeps as it struggled to free itself.

"Easy, now," Josh said, trying to calm the frightened animal.

"Here's the problem," the old man said, feeling along the wing.

"Can you fix it?" Josh asked.

"We can try," he said. "Hold him for a minute while I get some things."

16

He rummaged in a drawer and came back with some wooden matches and a spool of fishing line. After taking out his pocketknife, he broke the tips off the matches and cut a piece of line.

"Try to hold him still," he said.

The bird squawked loudly as the old man held the matches around the wing and started to wrap the line around it.

"Damn," he said after the matches had slipped out for the third time. "My hands seem to have a mind of their own these days." He stopped and rubbed his arthritic fingers. "You're going to have to finish this for me, son."

"Me? I don't know what to do," Josh said.

"Well, this is as good a time as any to learn," Mr. Davis told him, replacing the boy's hands on the bird with his own. "Hold the matches with one hand," he said. "Now, make a loop and wrap the line around the wing."

"Like this?" Josh asked.

"That's it."

The boy worked the string around the feathers, being careful not to break them.

"Now, tie it off by running the end through the loop and pulling it, just like tying a guide on a fishing rod."

He watched closely as Josh followed his instructions.

"There, that should do it," Mr. Davis said.

Josh stood back and examined his handiwork.

"Nice job, son," the old man said. "You must be quite a fisherman."

"I've only been once when my father took me," Josh said, blushing at the compliment.

Mr. Davis let go and the bird righted itself, folding its damaged wing as far as it could against its side. It sat on the table, looking at them sullenly.

"I think there's an old cage upstairs in the attic," Mr. Davis said. "Why don't you see if you can find it for me."

After rummaging around, Josh found the cage in the corner behind a stack of boxes.

"Got it," he said, holding it up as he walked back into the kitchen.

Mr. Davis took the cage over to the sink and cleaned it off while Josh sat looking at the little bird on the table. It had calmed down after the ordeal and cocked its head from side to side as it examined the room.

"This ought to do," the old man said, bringing the cage over to the table.

He swung open the door, and Josh carefully picked up the bird and put it on the perch inside.

"If you have a cat, you'll have to keep it away," Mr. Davis said as they watched it through the wire. "It'll drive the bird crazy."

"We don't have any pets," Josh said.

"Well, what do you think your mother will say about this?" he said, nodding at the bird.

"Oh, she won't mind. She loves animals," Josh told him, remembering for the first time his mother's edict against pets.

Mr. Davis held the door for Josh as he carried the cage to the car, then he closed it behind him and went into the den. As he rummaged through the shelves for a book to read, he heard the back door open again.

"Mr. Davis?"

He looked up and saw the boy standing there, holding his dinner.

"I almost forgot to give you this," Josh said apologetically.

"Just leave it on the table," he said, taking a book off the shelf.

Josh put down the container and turned to go, then stopped. "Mr. Davis?" The old man looked up from his book. "Thanks again."

"I just hope there's a happy ending," he said seriously as Josh turned to leave.

The old man watched out the window as the VW drove away. He stood there long after the car had disappeared around the bend, then put the book he was holding back on the shelf.

"You what?" Mrs. Bell said, looking at the rusty cage sitting on her kitchen table. "Josh, you know how I feel about pets. We just can't afford them."

"But he's not really a pet," Josh said convincingly. "He's a wild bird. I'm just going to keep him until his wing gets better, then I'll let him go."

"*I'm* not going to be the one feeding him and cleaning the cage," she said, not giving in easily.

"I'll do it," he said. "I promise."

She gave him a hard stare, then looked back over at the injured bird, her face softening some. "He is pretty," she said. "Look at how bright the blue on his back is, and I love that rusty color on his chest."

The bird puffed himself up as though he knew he was the subject of the conversation.

"Mr. Davis says they're very rare," Josh said, trying to sound knowledgeable on the subject.

"Well, it would be a shame just to let him die," she said, watching the little bird preen his feathers. "But you have to promise me that you'll let him go as soon as he's well."

"Deal," he said, picking up the cage to take it to his room.

"Just a minute," she said before he could slip away. She went into the kitchen and came back with a slice of bread. "See if he'll eat this until you can get him something tomorrow."

He put the cage on a table by the window, so the bird could see out during the day, then tore off a piece of bread and opened the door. The bird edged away from his hand to the end of the perch, then had nowhere else to go. Josh stroked his chest for a minute, then offered him the piece of bread, but he refused to eat. Josh scattered the rest of the bread on the bottom of the cage and went back to the kitchen.

When he came in later the bird was asleep, with his head tucked partly under his good wing. The bread in the cage was still untouched. Josh undressed quietly and slipped into bed, turning off the light. As his eyes adjusted to the dark, he could see the outline of the cage and the small shape huddled on the perch inside. He remembered what the old man had said and hoped there would be a happy ending, too.

Chapter 3

⁓

An Old-Fashioned Book Burning

As Josh stopped to make his last delivery, he saw Mr. Davis working in the flower bed that bordered the yard. He opened the back door to the house and left the dinner on the kitchen table. Then, letting the screen slam behind him, he walked across the wide lawn toward the old man. The azaleas in the yard were just beginning to bloom, and their delicate scent mixed with the smell of damp earth.

Mr. Davis knelt in the dirt with his back to him. Josh stood quietly and watched him work, noticing that the bulbs were pushing through here as they were in his mother's garden at home. The old man raked the ground with a pronged trowel, then carefully molded the dirt around each of the stalks. Finally Josh cleared his throat.

"I hear you, boy," he said without turning his head. "Would you interrupt a man kneeling in church?"

"No, sir," Josh answered uncertainly. "I

just wasn't sure you knew I was here," he added by way of explanation.

"I'm old, son, not deaf."

Mr. Davis leaned back on his heels, wiping his dirt-encrusted hands absently on his pants as he looked around him.

"In a way, this is a church," he said, gesturing with the trowel. "The roof is the limbs of these old oaks and the steeple the blue sky overhead. As for music, the rustling of the wind through the trees is more beautiful than any pipe organ I've ever heard." His arm sagged, and he looked down at the ground again. "It's days like this that make me sad that I'll be leaving all this behind soon."

"Are you going somewhere?" Josh asked innocently.

"We're all going somewhere," he said, glancing in the boy's direction, "it's more a question of when."

There was an awkward pause as Josh realized what he meant.

"Help me up, son," he said.

Josh took his arm as he struggled to his feet. Mr. Davis brushed the dirt off his pants, then put his hands on his back and stretched.

"It's not the kneeling that bothers me," he said with a grimace, "it's the getting up. If you've got a minute, I'll fix us something to drink and we'll go sit out on the wharf."

"Sure," Josh said, looking at his watch. "I'm actually early today for once."

They walked slowly back to the house as the old man worked the kinks out of his legs.

"How's our little feathered friend doing?" he asked.

"He seems fine, but he hasn't eaten anything yet," Josh said, sounding worried.

"Give him time. Maybe he'll come around once he gets used to his new home."

They climbed the back steps to the kitchen. Mr. Davis fixed their tea and handed a glass to Josh, then they walked through the house and down the front steps.

"What is it that you like to do most, Josh?" he asked as they strolled down the path to the water.

"That's easy," the boy said with a smile. "Surf."

"Surf? We didn't have that when I was growing up, though I was a pretty fair sailor in my day. I still have the little sailboat that I got when I was a boy. My best friend, John, and I must have covered about every inch of this bay in her. Kids on farms have a pony to keep them company, but here we had a boat."

The narrow wharf stretched far out into the bay, then widened into a boathouse and deck with a hip roof of rusty tin covering them both. On the roof's peak, a weather vane turned aimlessly in the light breeze, while two wooden Adirondack chairs faced out across the bay, waiting patiently.

Josh and Mr. Davis walked out on the wharf, the sound of their feet echoing up from the water below. The weathered boards were cracked and warped from years of exposure to the elements. Here and there one had been recently replaced, standing out in sharp contrast and giving the wharf the feel of a favorite old coat that's patched and frayed around the edges.

"My mother told me that this place has been in your family for a long time," Josh said.

"That's right. My grandfather built this house and the first wharf, too. This board," he said, pointing to a particularly worn and scarred plank, "is about all that's left of the original. When my father and I were rebuilding it after the 1916 hurricane, I found this piece all the way down by the road. When I turned it over, I noticed it had '1875' chiseled on the bottom. My grandfather must have dated it when he first built it. We put it back exactly halfway down the wharf as a reminder of the past." He bent over gingerly and rested his hand on it.

"Every time I look at it, I think of my father hammering it into place. I was twelve at the time, and I remember that he let me hit the last lick," he said nostalgically. "We must have done a good job, because it's stayed put through every storm since then."

"What's it like?" Josh asked.

"What? A hurricane?"

Josh nodded.

"You've lived here all your life and haven't been through one?"

"I was only in the third grade when Frederic hit," Josh said, "and we drove to Montgomery to get away from it. There haven't been any big ones since then."

"I guess you're right," he said, counting up

the years on his fingers. "It doesn't seem like it's been that long. Well, a hurricane is like nothing you can imagine. The storm that hit when I was a boy was one of the worst. You should have seen this place," he said, looking around him at the now tranquil scene. "The house was a wreck; it took months to repair. We lost a lot of the trees, and the wind blew almost all the leaves off the ones left standing. It hit in the middle of the summer, and it was strange to see them trying to put out new growth in the fall."

They continued down the wharf and sat in the chairs. Except for the hum of the breeze through the tin, it was quiet.

"I always feel better near the water," the old man said. "It's so deep and mysterious. We only see the surface, but there's a whole other world underneath. It's where we came from, and where I plan to return."

"Return?" Josh asked.

"When the time comes, I want to be cremated and sprinkled in the bay off the end of this wharf," he said, nodding toward the dark water. "The Bible says dust to dust, but that's just because they were a desert people."

They sat quietly for a minute.

"It's so peaceful out here, I can see why you feel that way," Josh said.

"It is, isn't it. I can sit here by the hour just reflecting on life. In fact, there's a saying that I've been giving a lot of thought to lately," he said, weighing his words carefully. "'When an old man dies, a library burns to the ground.'"

He paused to let the words sink in.

"You see, Josh, all your life you're storing up memories of people, places, and lessons you've learned. If you boil it all down, what you have left in the bottom of the pot is wisdom. Sometimes it takes a lifetime to make sense out of what you've learned. Then, if you have the ability to express yourself in words, you can make a lasting gift of it to the world."

"Kind of like saving some of the books in the library before they can burn," Josh added, his eyes briefly meeting the old man's.

"Exactly," Mr. Davis said, impressed by the boy's insight. "Do you know how old I am?"

Josh tried to quickly do the math in his head, then gave up. "No, sir."

"I'm eighty-four years old. That's eighty-four springs like this one that I've seen. And in all those years I've tried to take the time to look beyond the surface of the world and deep into its heart. And do you know what's at that heart?"

The boy shook his head, not wanting to interrupt him.

"Stories, Josh, a thousand different stories. If you take away all the books, you take away the heart of humanity." He leaned forward, resting his hands on his knees. "I've lived a full life, but I've yet to tell the stories that are in *my* heart. I have a problem, though."

"What's that?" Josh asked, his curiosity getting the better of him.

"My arthritis has gotten so bad that I have

a hard time writing," he said, flexing his stiff fingers. "So I have a proposition for you. I want you to be my hands."

"I don't get it," Josh said, looking at him with a puzzled expression.

"I want you to write down my stories for me," Mr. Davis said, clarifying his words.

"I don't know—"

"I'll pay you, of course. We could work on it a little every afternoon when you drop off my supper."

"It's not that. It's just that I have a lot to do with graduation coming up and all."

"Give it a try for a week. If it doesn't work out, then no hard feelings."

"Well..."

"You would be doing me a big favor."

Josh was silent for a minute as he turned the offer over in his head.

"Okay," he said.

"Good."

"Exactly what do you want me to do?"

"I'll talk, you write. It's as simple as that."

"But what are you going to do with it when we're through?" Josh questioned.

"That's not really important. What's important is getting it done," Mr. Davis answered, neatly sidestepping his question.

"Is this going to be the story of your life, or something you're going to make up?" he asked.

"Well, I guess that depends on how you look at it," the old man said, taking a sip of tea. "How I remember my life is not the same way someone else would have seen it."

"What do you mean? Either something happened or it didn't," Josh said.

"It's not that simple, son. Memories are tricky things. Everything we experience is filtered through our mind, and what comes out the other side has been transformed. Everybody sees things a little differently. That's the interesting thing about books; they let you catch a glimpse of the world through someone else's eyes." He paused, searching for a comparison the boy could understand. "If I went to the beach, I would just see a wave, but you would see something else. The angle it was breaking, the shape and form of it, would all mean something different to you."

Josh's eyes lit up. "The first thing I do is sit for a while just watching the waves break before I ever go in the water," he said. "I imagine myself riding each one and watch to see where the good spots are that day."

"That's what I'm talking about," Mr. Davis said. "Every work of fiction is influenced by what the author has seen and felt, and every autobiography is partly fiction whether it's meant to be or not. There's not a wall between the two, they just blend into each other like the bay meeting the gulf," he said, gesturing to the water around them. "Besides, I'm planning to hold truth to a higher standard than mere fact. So let's just say that this is my book of stories and leave it at that."

The afternoon breeze had died completely now, and the bay was calm and still. A flock of pelicans winged their way along the shore.

"It's getting late," Mr. Davis said, rising slowly from his chair. "You need to get home, and I've got my supper to eat."

They walked side by side back down the wharf toward the house.

"Take the weekend off, and we'll start fresh on Monday," he said as they parted company at the steps.

"Okay. I'll see you then," Josh said over his shoulder.

As he drove home down the winding road that followed the contours of the bay, Josh thought about what the old man had said. The road into town left the coastline and straightened out before him. He gave the tired engine more gas and watched the familiar houses slip by on either side. Ahead, the streetlights began to click on one by one, as if to light his way.

"Are you sure you want to do this, Josh?" Mrs. Bell said as they finished dinner. "You don't have to."

"I know, but I'd like to give it a try. Besides, we could use the money."

"You should be out with your friends more," she said guiltily, "not cooped up with someone five times your age." The pain of their financial difficulties was written plainly on her face.

"There's nothing to do after school anyway but hang out at the park," he said to reassure her.

"But what about school?"

"I can keep up. It might not work out. I'm just going to try it for a week."

"Well, I guess so if your grades don't drop. You've still got a chance at a scholarship."

"I know," Josh said as he started clearing the table.

Later he went out to the car and brought in the bag of birdseed that he had bought. When he opened the door to his room, the bluebird was sitting quietly on its perch. The pieces of bread on the bottom of the cage were now littered with droppings. Josh changed the newspaper and filled a jar lid with seed, sliding it in the cage next to the dish of water. He watched the bird for a minute, hoping for any sign of change.

"You've got to eat something," he said, pleading. But the bird just stared at him silently.

Chapter 4

Footsteps

Eat up. I've got another batch cooking," Mrs. Bell said as she slid the spatula under the pancakes and flipped them.

"Give me a minute, I'm almost ready," Josh answered, stuffing the last bite in his mouth.

The ritual of Saturday morning pancakes went back as far as he could remember. Even back to the time when she was cooking for more than just the two of them. She brought the pan over to the kitchen table and scooped the hot stack onto his empty plate. Josh lifted them one by one with his fork, trying not to burn his fingers as he buttered them, then drenched the whole pile with syrup. He cut a large triangular bite and chewed contentedly.

"And don't stay all day in the shower," she said. "You don't want to be late."

She turned off the stove and started washing out the mixing bowls in the sink.

"When am I supposed to meet him?" he asked.

"He said he would be at the park around twelve."

"So why do you think he called?"

"He's your father. Does he need a reason to call?"

"You can do better than that," Josh admonished her.

"All he said was that he wanted to see you. He's probably just wondering how you are."

"Right," he said.

"What?" she asked, turning off the water and facing him.

"He hasn't wondered before, why now?"

"Well," she said, hesitating, "it's a big year for you, with graduation and all, and he's got a lot of catching up to do. Don't you want to see him?"

"I guess so," Josh answered slowly. He finished the last bite and carried his plate over to the sink. "It's just that I've finally written him off, and now he wants to show up like nothing ever happened."

"Everyone has to start somewhere," she said, taking his plate and rinsing it in the sink. "Now, hurry up and get dressed so you can help me make a lunch for you to take."

He stood looking at her back for a minute, then walked away. She turned off the water and listened as his footsteps disappeared down the hall.

Josh pulled into an empty space in the parking lot and turned off the engine, then sat in the car, looking out over the town park at the public pier. In the early days it had provided the only link to the city of Mobile on the other side of the bay, and it was constantly busy as boats docked and unloaded. The early wooden pier had been replaced by the present concrete one, and today it served more as a recreational and tourist attraction than a necessity. Sightseers strolled along, and he could see a few fishermen and crabbers leaning against the railing, hoping for the first catch of the season. The park had been set aside when the town was founded, which was fortunate since every other square foot of usable real estate along the bay had long since been developed.

Josh got out and walked over to one of the picnic tables that were scattered under the trees. He passed an older couple standing on the arched footbridge, throwing bread to the ducks in the stream below. The ducks raced through the water after each piece, clamoring for another handout.

He sat down with his back to the table and rested his elbows on it, watching the people around him while he waited. It was a hobby of his, observing people the way others watched birds. He made a game of it, trying to construct the story of their lives from the few visible fragments that he could see.

He watched a family at a table near him. The father was gently tossing a ball underhand to his young son, who held an oversize glove out before him. Occasionally the ball actually landed in it, and the father would clap and cheer while the boy grinned broadly. Then he would fish it out of the glove and throw it wildly back to him. The boy's mother was busy spreading their lunch on the table and looked up at the sound, following their progress closely. It was an idyllic scene, but he wondered if anyone could really be that happy.

After a minute Josh looked away and focused his attention on a freighter plowing slowly up the bay. He could see Mobile beyond it in the hazy distance, and not for the first time he pondered the enigma that was his father. The man he had looked up to more than anyone else in the world, who for so long could do no wrong in his eyes and now seemed incapable of doing anything right. Maybe today would change all that, he thought.

Josh heard a squeal and turned to see a

boy on the pier with a catfish dangling off the end of his rod. He swung the fish around in a wide circle, unsure what to do next. The man standing next to the boy said something, and he stopped and held the rod still. The man took the line in one hand and carefully unhooked the fish, avoiding the sharp fins. He held it out to the boy, and after a little coaxing, the boy reached out and touched the fish, which elicited another shriek of delight.

Watching them reminded Josh of the time his father had taken him fishing here. His aunt in Mobile had given him a rod and reel for Christmas, and he had begged his father for weeks to take him. Finally the weather warmed up enough, and they got up early one Saturday morning and drove to the pier.

"Now, I'm only going to show you one time," his father said, holding the hook and a dead shrimp in front of the boy's face.

A cigarette dangled out of the corner of his mouth, and Josh saw him squint as the smoke blew back in his eyes. He watched as his father ran the hook through the shrimp and threaded it on, following the curve of its body.

"Think you can do that next time?" he asked.

Josh nodded, already unsure which end went on first.

"To cast you hold this button down, then let it go when you bring it forward."

He swung the rod around, and Josh watched the shrimp and weight sail through the air, landing with a plop in the dark water off the pier.

"Okay, you hold it and let me know if you feel anything," he said, handing the rod to the boy.

Josh held it stiffly in his hands, afraid to move for fear of scaring away the fish. His father leaned on the railing next to him and took another drag on his cigarette.

"I bought you something when I was in Atlanta this week," he said after they had stared at the water in silence for a few minutes.

"You did?" Josh said, surprised.

He nodded and reached in his pocket, pulling out a small wrapped box.

"What is it?" Josh asked, his rod forgotten as he strained impatiently to see.

His father handed him the package, and Josh put down his rod, leaning it against the railing.

The boy tore off the wrapping paper and looked at the small black jeweler's box.

"You have to open it," his father said with a smile.

Josh rolled his eyes. "I know," he said, prying it open. He stared down at the filigreed chain nestled around a small silver medal that bore the imprint of a man with a staff carrying a small child on his shoulders.

"It's a Saint Christopher medal," his father told him in response to his questioning look.

"Oh," Josh said, holding up the box to look at it closely. "Who was he?"

"Well, he was a ferryman on a river a long time ago. It was his job to carry people safely to the other side. One day a child appeared and asked to be taken across. As he carried him on his shoulders, the child seemed to get heavier and heavier with every step, until he could barely stand. When they had finally reached the other shore safely, the child revealed himself as Jesus. He blessed Christopher, telling him that he had carried the weight of the entire world on his shoulders."

His father took it out of the box and fastened it around Josh's neck. "If you wear it, it's supposed to protect you from harm and bring you good luck."

Josh turned the medal around in his fingers, looked at it, and smiled up at him. The rod clattered on the pier next to him, and Josh grabbed it just as it was about to be pulled over the railing.

"See, it's working already," his father said with a laugh as Josh struggled to reel in the fish.

Josh watched the man on the pier throw the catfish back over the side while he fingered the medal that hadn't left his neck since that day. It hadn't worked so well after all, he thought cynically, since it wasn't much later that the trouble first started. He still remembered clearly the long nights of barely audible arguments, while he lay in his bed feigning sleep. He was too young to fully understand the intricacies of the complex dance that two people must engage in if a marriage is to succeed, but he was old enough to know something wasn't right. Then one night the back door didn't open, and the house remained quiet. His mother stayed in her room while he played listlessly with his toys and watched out the window for the sweep of headlights that would never come.

He's on his way here, Josh thought with an odd mixture of anticipation and dread. He imagined his father closing the front door to the house in the city that he shared with his new wife and young children. He knew the outside of it well, having driven by without stopping half a dozen times since he had gotten his driver's license. The house was like a magnet that drew him to the place he had never been invited, the place his father now called home.

Josh looked at his watch: after twelve. He sat tapping his foot nervously as he scanned each car that drove into the park. Finally he took the book Mr. Davis had loaned him out of his pocket and began to read to pass the time. Soon he was immersed in the story of the old fisherman, and thoughts of his father slipped away as the words formed images in his mind.

He didn't see the car pull up next to his in the parking lot and didn't hear the door close quietly or the footsteps behind him. He just felt the hand on his shoulder and looked up into the eyes that he knew so well, eyes that he had always loved and always would. They returned his gaze, and he felt a hollowness forming in the pit of his stomach.

"He's not coming, is he," Josh said matter-of-factly, trying to clear his voice of emotion and pretending that this was the inevitable consequence he had expected all along.

"No," his mother replied softly. "He called to say that something came up, that he would try to make it again soon."

Josh sighed and looked back at the skyline in the distance. He was seeing the house again, the door still tightly shut.

"I knew he wouldn't," he said, sliding off the table and walking down toward the bay.

She let him go and watched him stand on the beach skipping stones one after another across the water, his back turned to her. A sharp pain went through her, but she willed her feet not to move. She waited until the tension left his shoulders and the rocks he threw plunked harmlessly in the shallow water at his feet, then she walked down beside him and again put her hand on his shoulder. She knew that there was nothing she could say and that anything she did say would be wrong. The little boy that she could rock so tightly and make every hurt go away had grown up, and nothing she could do would make the pain disappear.

"We might as well eat lunch," she said, giving his arm a pat. "Then I'll buy you an ice-cream cone out on the pier just like we used to."

He continued to stare off into the distance for a minute, then turned and looked at her with a sad smile.

"Sure."

They walked slowly back to the picnic table.

She opened the basket, got out two plates, and started fixing them.

Josh sat quietly at the table, still staring out across the bay. In the distance the haze from the city shimmered in the light, successfully hiding the far shore from view.

Chapter 5

A Thin Line

Over the weekend Josh finished *The Old Man and the Sea* and brought it with him to return to Mr. Davis on Monday. Another cold front had moved in that morning, causing the temperature to drop. As he pulled up the drive to the old man's house, tree limbs whipped back and forth in the strong wind that was blowing across the bay. Clouds hung low over the water, propelled along by the wind.

He arrived in the midst of a sudden downpour and parked close to the steps. Turning off the engine, he looked at the back door and calculated the degree of soaking that would be involved in making a dash for the house. The rain came down even harder, and he decided to wait it out. He passed the time listening to the radio and drawing faces on the fogged windshield.

Finally the rain began to let up. He tucked

the book into the waistband of his jeans and zipped up his jacket around it, then forced the car door open against the wind. After taking the container off the seat, he hurried up the steps and in the back door, closing it quickly behind him. He put the food on the table and took off his jacket, which was already soaked from the ten other stops he had made, and hung it on a hook by the door.

Mr. Davis was reading in his recliner in the den. A fire burned brightly in the fireplace to ward off the chill of the day.

"Come in and warm yourself," he called to the boy.

Josh handed him the book. "I finished this over the weekend," he said, backing up next to the fire.

"Well, what did you think?" Mr. Davis asked.

"It was good," he said. "I really felt like I knew the old fisherman and what his life was like. But..." He paused, unsure of himself.

"But what?"

"It was so sad," he continued. "I mean, in the end the old man had nothing."

"He had his honor, and he stood strong in the face of adversity," Mr. Davis countered.

"But he could barely walk, and his hands were cut to ribbons," Josh said, shaking his head.

"Well, he regained the respect of his village," he said.

"But they could turn against him again if he doesn't catch anything else."

"He won the boy back," Mr. Davis said. "He has his love."

"Yes, that is something," Josh answered, thinking it over. "But the boy loved him anyway. He would have been better off catching a smaller fish and making it home with it."

"Would he? That's not the way of men. We're born to bite off more than we can chew."

"But when he finally caught something big, something that would show the world how great a fisherman he was, it was taken away from him."

Mr. Davis gave the boy a sad smile. "Irony is never buried very deep, Josh. We've never been able to understand that the world doesn't revolve around us—it just revolves."

He pulled his recliner upright and indicated a chair next to him. Josh sat down facing the fire.

"Let me tell you a story that happened to me when I was a boy growing up here. A lesson life taught me that I've never forgotten."

He reached over to the table next to him and handed Josh a spiral notebook and pen.

"Speak up if I go too fast," he said.

Josh nodded, opening the notebook to the first page. Mr. Davis leaned back in his chair and stared into the fire.

"I was twelve years old at the time, the year of the big storm. But the story I'm about to tell you occurred earlier that summer, and the hurricane that would lay waste to this area was still just a swirl of wind somewhere far out in the ocean. My best friend, John, and

I spent just about every day that summer fishing or sailing on the bay."

Josh balanced the notebook on his knee as he wrote.

"Living here was paradise," the old man continued. "Long summer days with nothing to do but be a boy...."

The boy stood at the kitchen table, packing a picnic lunch in the early morning light. He carefully wrapped waxed paper around the fried chicken, hard-boiled eggs, and chocolate-chip cookies that his mother had made the day before. Then he put everything in a wicker basket that lay open next to him. He took a pitcher of tea out of the icebox and filled a quart canning jar, spilling some on the table and wiping it up with a dishtowel. His mother came in just as he was finishing up.

"Be careful today, Will," she said, adding a couple of apples to the basket from the bowl of fruit in the center of the table.

"I will," he said as he picked up the basket and turned to leave.

"Don't be home late. You know how I worry."

"Yes, ma'am," he said, slamming the screen door behind him.

After grabbing the fishing rod that leaned against the porch, he walked down the front steps and stopped to look out over the bay. The sun sparkled off the ripples stirred up by the first sign of a morning breeze. He walked down the hill from the house and out on the wharf to the sailboat that bobbed gently up and down. Once on board, he stored the lunch basket under the enclosed bow, then readied the sails. Footsteps sounded on the wharf, and he turned to see John running toward him.

"Glad to see you could make it," Will said at his friend's tardiness.

"Are you kidding?" John replied, taking the remark at face value. "You know I'll always be here when we can go fishing."

He handed Will his rod and tackle box, then climbed into the boat and began untying the ropes that held it fast to the pier.

"Hey, this might be our lucky day!" John added. "Maybe we'll hook that big tarpon everybody's been talking about."

"He didn't get that big by being caught," Will said, pushing them away from the dock.

When they were clear of the wharf, John raised the sail and Will pulled in the mainsheet. He turned the boat to gather the breeze while John busied himself with the jib. They sailed south, following the coastline, then steered the boat toward a deserted stretch of beach. John pulled up the centerboard, and they slid up to within a few feet of the shore. Will let go of the mainsheet, allowing the boom to swing out until it pointed into the wind with the sails luffing.

They hopped over the side, splashing in the warm water. Will reached under the bow and pulled out his cast net, looping the end of the line securely over his wrist. Holding the

43

coiled rope in his one hand, he flipped part of the net over his forearm and gripped the weighted bottom line in his teeth. Then, wading quietly in the shallow water, he looked for mullet. John followed closely behind, carrying a croaker sack to keep their catch. When Will spotted a school swimming near the surface, he would throw the net with all his strength in their direction.

A skilled man throwing a cast net is a beautiful sight to see. He stands poised in water up to his waist: watching...waiting. Then, in one fluid motion, everything tightens, coils back, and is propelled forward. The net sails out effortlessly, and the weighted bottom line arcs through the air, spreading into a perfect circle of enormous proportions. It splashes uniformly in the water and sinks slowly to the bottom. When he is sure the net has settled, he pulls it in, drawing the bottom line together and trapping any fish inside.

In the hands of boys with small nets, the outcome is not nearly so dramatic. Often the result is a tangle of lines and misshapen ovals that splash loudly in the water and do little but frighten the fish. After an hour of diligent effort, several mullet managed to swim into the net and the boys had enough to use for bait. They tied a rope to the sack and suspended it over the side in the water to keep the fish alive, then pushed the boat away from the shore. After climbing in over the transom, they headed back out into the bay.

Half a mile from shore, Will turned the

bow into the wind while John lowered the sails. They each hooked a mullet through the tail and let their lines out on opposite sides of the boat. The fish swam away in different directions in a futile attempt at escape.

There was nothing to do now but wait. They stretched out, holding their rods loosely in their laps, and relaxed. They talked—as boys will—about places they wanted to go and people they hoped to meet. They had spent many a rainy afternoon curled up with books from Will's father's library, absorbed in a world of Tom and Huck and steamboats on the mighty Mississippi, or brave Jim Hawkins and Long John Silver headed for an island full of treasure. In their imaginations the world was still filled with tall-masted schooners and treacherous pirates.

"I thought we might sail to the mouth of the bay this summer and camp out for a few days," Will said. "We could explore the old Civil War fort there."

"They'll never let us go," John replied.

"We can try, can't we? We'll just have to talk them into it."

"I've heard there's an old hermit who lives out there," John said, pulling on his line to be sure he still had bait.

"No one could live out there without fresh water," Will said.

"Maybe he collects rainwater or something."

"I doubt it," Will scoffed.

"I don't know. I heard one of the shrimpers

say that they saw someone standing on the shore when they were going out through the channel." John tensed as he thought he felt something on his line.

"I think he was just pulling your leg."

"He sounded like he meant it to me," John countered, jerking his rod only to realize that it was just the pull of the tide. "Well, it sounds like fun if they'll let us. Nobody ever goes out there, so it would almost be like we were on a deserted island."

"We would be the only ones around for miles."

"Yeah, just like *Robinson Crusoe* or *The Swiss Family Robinson*," John fantasized.

"We could look for stuff that washed up on the beach, too," Will said. "You never know what you might find."

"Like that pirate treasure that's supposed to be buried on Dauphin Island," John added excitedly.

They opened their lunch and ate while the boat drifted slowly with the tide. As the warm sun poured down, their talk tapered off and finally ceased altogether, and they dozed peacefully while the breeze pushed them farther out into the bay.

There was an almost imperceptible tightening on Will's line. The tip twitched slightly, then went slack again. The boys dozed on, unaware. The line tightened a second time, and Will opened his eyes and looked at his rod. Probably just a snag on the bottom, he thought as he pulled on the line.

Suddenly the rod bent double with a force that bashed his left hand hard against the rail of the boat. The line sang from the reel as the drag worked overtime to slow the first run of the fish. The boat tipped precariously to one side, its gunwale almost touching the water. Only the counterbalance of the centerboard kept it from turning over completely. John—still groggy—slid off his seat, bumping his head on the centerboard trunk.

Will tried frantically to balance both fish and boat as the bow swung around in the direction the line was heading. He moved closer to the bow, partly to stabilize the boat and partly from the sheer force placed on the rod he held tightly in his hands. His left hand was throbbing, and it took a conscious effort to maintain his grip on the rod. He tightened the drag as much as he dared, but still the line was going out at an alarming rate. Soon it would reach the end of the spool and snap under the strain. The small boat started to move slowly forward through the water, pulled by the powerful fish.

"Fight him, Will!" John called from the bottom of the boat as he tried to sit up.

"I am!" Will answered between clenched teeth.

"Don't let him get off!" he said, reeling in his rod to keep their lines from fouling.

"I'm trying!" Will yelled in response.

"You've got to slow him down or you'll lose him for sure!"

Will looked at the rapidly revolving reel. A

thin wisp of smoke curled up from inside, and he could see the bare metal of the spool as the last few yards of line played out. Then, as suddenly as it began, the line went slack. He thought for sure it had broken, but when he looked down at the lifeless reel, there were still a few feet of line left on it. He looked over at John, and their eyes met.

"I guess you lost him," John said, disappointment filling his voice.

Before the words had left his lips, Will saw the water in front of the boat begin to swirl. He leaned over the side and watched as the bay before him began to churn and boil. Then the bay parted cleanly, and the tarpon burst through the surface. Up and up it rose until it towered over the small boat. The great fish seemed to hang suspended in midair—water pouring off its silver scales. Its eye stared down at him as if sizing up its adversary. Will could see the hook and line clearly visible in its open mouth as the fish shook its massive head violently from side to side in an effort to free itself. Then it hit the water with a booming splash that sent a shower of spray cascading over them, rocking the boat dangerously.

"Reel!" John screamed.

Will, who had been transfixed by the sight, began frantically to take up the slack left in the line when the fish had doubled back toward the boat. He managed to partly fill the spool before the next run came. It was as violent as the first, but he was ready for it this time. He leaned back on the rod, bracing his feet against the forward compartment, and fought for all he was worth. Once again the boat surged through the water as it was towed out into the bay. For the second time the silver king leaped, reaching toward the heavens and shaking its head against the hook. This time Will seized the opportunity to take up slack and shorten the distance between them.

The numbing pull on the line resumed, settling down into a relentless, backbreaking fight as the tarpon sounded. This was the hardest time of all, pitting the raw strength of the fish against the pure determination of the boy. Will's arms ached under the strain, and the pain in his hand had increased. He managed to tighten the drag a little more, so that very little line was leaving the reel.

The battle had begun in earnest. Time seemed to slow down until he could hear the ticking of each second in the pulse of blood through his temples. The boat was heading farther and farther out, and Will could feel the strength sapping from his arms and legs. He was losing the feeling in his fingers, but the fish continued its constant pressure. He thought about handing the rod over to John, but two against one didn't seem fair. This battle was just between them and no one else.

Eventually the boat slowed and the pull lessened. Will leaned back on the rod as far as he could, then lowered it quickly and reeled, managing to take in a little line. Again and again he pulled, gaining a few precious inches each time. The line began to angle straighter down into the water as he steadily closed the gap. Then only a few yards separated them, and the fish began to circle the boat. Will had to work to keep the line from fouling as he shifted around the mast.

As he took up the last few feet of line, the huge creature became visible. At first it was only a lighter streak in the dark water of the bay. Then its outline began to take shape, and he could see the fish rolling on its side just under the surface. Its mouth moved back and forth silently, and the eye again looked at the boy.

Will stared at the fish. They seemed bound together by the thin line, and he found it hard to tell where one ended and the other began. He could feel the call of the sea flowing through his veins and the weightless freedom the water gave. He was drawn down into the body of the fish, felt the tug of the watery depths and the sharp pull of the hook.

"You've got him, Will!" John said triumphantly. "He's ours now!"

"No..." Will muttered softly.

"What? Bring him up a little more and I'll run a rope through his gills."

"No," he repeated, more forcefully this time.

Will pulled out his pocketknife and managed to work it open with the numb fingers of one hand. He brought the blade slowly toward the taut line.

"Will? What are you doing?" John said, unable to believe his eyes.

The sharp steel touched the line gently,

like a loving kiss, and it parted cleanly. For a moment the fish stayed suspended near the surface, its eye still fixed impassively on the boy, then it slowly sank out of sight into the murky depths of the bay.

"Are you crazy? We had him! We had him right here at the boat," John said, furious. "No one around here has caught one that big! It might even have been a record, and you let him go?"

"Yes," Will said evenly.

"But why?"

Will sat with his head bowed for a long time before he spoke, while the boat rocked calmly in the waning light.

"You remember that time we collected butterflies?" he finally said, looking up.

"Yeah, sure," John answered impatiently.

"They were so beautiful," Will said. "We would catch them in our nets and mount them in boxes under glass."

"So?"

"I used to sit and look at them in my room, but it wasn't the same. Not like watching them land on a flower in the yard, seeing them sit there with their wings slowly opening and closing."

"I don't get it," John said.

"I guess what I'm trying to say is that some things are better off left alone," Will said, knowing that his words could never express what he felt deep inside. "Sometimes it's enough just to know that they're out there somewhere."

51

They sat silently as the sun dropped low in the sky. John looked over at Will and started to say something, then he shook his head and turned to raise the sails. Will watched them fill with the breeze and pointed the boat toward the green mass of the distant shore.

It was late when they reached the wharf. John tied up the boat while Will stowed away their gear. After they had finished, the boys walked down the wharf together. Halfway down it, Will stopped and turned to his friend.

"Let's not tell anyone about the fish," he said.

"Why not?"

"Because they wouldn't understand."

"I'm not sure *I* understand," John replied.

"Just do it for me."

John hesitated. "Okay," he said.

They parted company at the end of the wharf, and Will climbed up the hill to the house. He left his rod on the porch and walked into the kitchen, putting the empty basket in the corner. His father was sitting at the table, reading the paper, while his mother stirred a pot on the stove.

"You're home late," she said, relieved to see him.

"We were out farther than I thought," Will answered quietly.

"Any luck?" his father asked over the top of the paper.

Will shrugged. "Depends on what you call luck."

"Well, where I come from, luck is considered catching fish."

"Then we didn't have any," Will replied without elaborating.

"What about the big one that got away?" his father said with a smile.

Will looked over at him, a serious expression on his face. "Maybe sometimes it's better *if* the big one gets away," he said, turning to go upstairs to his room.

His parents glanced at each other, not knowing what to make of his remark.

As Will lay in his bed that night, looking out the open window at the stars flung across the sky, sleep wouldn't come. His arms ached, and he thought of the fish somewhere out in the bay, moving slowly through the dark water. Again he saw the eye that had plumbed the depths of his soul, and he tried to sift through his feelings. Then he realized what it was. It was not just the people close to him he loved, but the whole world as well. Fish, tree, bay, and sky seemed to fuse together as one, and he felt himself floating off into the night like a balloon, the earth growing smaller and smaller in the distance until it was just a twinkling point of light like the stars overhead. He rolled over on his side and closed his eyes, comforted by the presence of the bay close outside his window as he drifted off to sleep.

The rain had stopped falling and darkness had settled in by the time Mr. Davis finished telling his story. Neither of them spoke as they sat in the dim light of the den, their eyes drawn to the glowing coals in the fireplace. Josh could still hear the wind outside as it swirled around the house, but it sighed softly now, lacking the raw power that it had possessed before. After a few minutes he closed the notebook and quietly let himself out the back door. Mr. Davis didn't even look up as he left. He was still lost in his memories, his eyes staring deeply into the dying embers.

Outside it had turned colder. Josh zipped up his coat as he walked down the steps, then looked up at the night sky. The clouds were breaking up, and he could see stars beginning to emerge. He walked around the corner of the house and leaned against the trunk of an oak as he looked out across the bay.

Josh thought about the old man sitting alone inside by the fire. What will I look back on and remember? he wondered. What stories will I have to tell? The story of the fish seemed so clear and simple, he thought, while my life is anything but.

As he watched, the moon broke through the tattered remnants of clouds. It rode low in the west, its light reflecting off the water to illuminate the bay.

He walked back to his car and started it up, swinging around in a tight circle. His headlights cut through the darkness as he drove away, casting elongated shadows from the trees that lined the drive.

Chapter 6

─────── ∽ ───────

Letters Home

It's a beautiful day outside, so rise and shine, you sleepyheads, it's time to rock and roll! This is WBCH 96 FM, and it's six-thirty in the A.M.! How about a little wake-up music to get you going!" A rooster crowed, and the Beatles launched into "Good Morning, Good Morning."

Josh reached over and hit the snooze button on the clock radio next to his bed, then rolled back over. He had dreamed about the tarpon, weaving the story together with the book the old man had loaned him.

"Josh," his mother called down the hall, "are you up yet?"

He tried to chase the thoughts away, since they didn't make the prospect of being locked up in a classroom all day any easier.

"I have to leave for work now," she said, knocking on his bedroom door. "Are you up?"

"I'm up," he said, rolling over and looking at the clock. He sat up in bed, rubbing his eyes with the palms of his hands.

"Don't forget to take the garbage to the street before you leave for school," she said, waiting patiently for an answer. "Josh? Did you hear me?"

"I heard!" he snapped, regretting it almost immediately.

There was a long pause, followed by the sharp click of her shoes on the hardwood floor, and he heard the back door close. He lay there alone for a minute, then dragged himself out of bed and into the shower.

"Hey, Josh, I hear it's gonna be up this weekend. Are you coming?" Chris asked as he plopped his tray across from Josh and swung a leg over the chair back.

The cafeteria was its usual high-decibel blend of order and chaos. Josh sat at a table with half a dozen other surfers, and as usual the topic was waves.

"I'm thinking about it," he replied.

"What about the jetty? We haven't been there for a while," Chris said, eagerly digging into his hamburger and fries.

Josh sat poised with the ketchup bottle in one hand and the bun of his hamburger in the other. He looked down at the rubbery patty of meat on his plate with a pained expression.

"What *is* this?" he asked, poking the boy next to him with an elbow and indicating his plate.

Mark glanced over at it, then looked away. "Don't start on that again," he replied between bites. "I happen to like this stuff until you start dissecting it."

"So Saturday at the jetty, right?" Chris asked again.

"Sure," Josh said, burying his burger under a deluge of ketchup.

"Hey, remember when we were there last fall, just after that big storm came through?" Mark said to keep the subject away from food. "I'll bet the waves were six feet at least."

"More like four," Josh replied, taking a bite and chewing it warily. "I keep telling you that waves are measured from the back side, not the face."

"Well, whatever, Mr. Expert," Mark said. "They were still impressive anyway."

Josh made a face and stopped chewing, then fished a piece of gristle out of his mouth and held it out for Mark to see.

"What is *this?*" he asked again.

Mark looked the other way, humming loudly to drown him out. The bell rang, and Josh took his tray to the window, dumping the barely eaten food in the trash.

His ninth delivery kept him longer than usual. Mrs. Howard always talked nonstop, but today she had a window that wouldn't open and asked Josh if he would mind looking at it.

"It opened last fall," she said in a shaky voice. "I just know it did. I distinctly remember opening it to hear the birds at my feeder."

"Yes, ma'am," Josh said, pulling on the window handles.

"Did I tell you that I got a new feeder, Josh?" she said, pointing out the window at it. "The old one just fell apart. First the perch broke, then the little hook that held it up gave way, and the next thing I knew the whole thing hit the ground and broke into a million pieces. It nearly scared Precious to death."

She picked up the overweight cat that had been sitting on the table.

"Yes, ma'am." He pulled harder on the handles.

"You know what I think? I think those pesky squirrels did it," she said, leaning around Josh and rapping on the window at a squirrel sitting on a branch nearby.

"Did what?" Josh asked, not following the one-sided conversation.

"Broke my feeder, of course. You should see them running my poor birds away. Once, the squirrels got so bad that I took the screen out and sat by the window all day long with a garden hose. Every time they came around, I'd let them have it. They didn't like that at all," she said with a smile. "I know it sounds cruel," she added quickly, worried what he might think of her, "but they were running all my poor birds away. My son, Edward, put the new feeder up for me. He said, 'Mother, now you just leave those squirrels alone.'"

"Yes, ma'am." Josh began to examine the window, looking for the problem.

"Maybe it's all this rainy weather we've been having," she continued, barely pausing to breathe. "I just don't know what I'm going to do if it doesn't stop soon."

"Yes, ma'am."

Josh noticed that the sash lock was securely

in place. He turned it, pulled, and the window slid up easily.

"Oh, Josh, you fixed it! I knew you could. I said to Precious just this morning that if anyone can fix my window, Josh can. I can't let her outside, though; she's harder on the birds than the squirrels are. Why, just yesterday I caught her at the window staring at my birds with only one thing on her mind. I just don't know where she gets it from. If I've told her once, I've told her—"

"It was just the lock, Mrs. Howard," Josh said. "You have to unlock it before you open it."

"Oh, silly me. I didn't even think to check the lock! What would I do without you, Josh?"

"No problem," Josh said, backing toward the door before she could get wound up again.

"Let me get you something for helping me," she said, putting the cat down and picking up her purse.

"That's all right," Josh said, opening the door. "It was no trouble at all."

"I insist, Josh. I just don't know what I would do without you. Edward lives all the way over in Mobile and hardly ever comes by to see me. When he does come, he can only stay a minute. He just hasn't got the time, he says. Edward's a lawyer, you know. They made him a partner in his firm this year," she said in a proud voice. She closed her purse and held a dollar bill out to him.

"I really didn't mind," he said, stepping out onto the landing.

"Joshua, you take it this instant or I won't be able to sleep tonight. It's the least I can do." She handed him the bill, which he accepted reluctantly.

"Thanks," he said, turning to go.

"Are you sure you won't have something to drink? I have Coke and Pepsi and a little lemonade and—"

"Thanks anyway, Mrs. Howard, but I've still got a few more deliveries to make."

He walked quickly down the steps as she rummaged through her mind for something else to make him stay a little longer. "What about some cake? I made it just yesterday. Yellow cake with chocolate icing. Your favorite, Josh."

"I've really got to be going."

He was at the car now, opening the door as he waved good-bye.

"Are you sure? I've got ice cream, too. It will only take a minute to—"

He started up the engine and waved once more while backing out of the driveway. She waved back as she watched him drive away, then turned and looked around the kitchen for something else to occupy her. She picked up the cat, which was rubbing against her legs, and carried it to her chair by the window, where she sat petting it as it purred contentedly.

"Oh, Precious, I forgot to show him the screen door that's been sticking," she said, staring out the window vacantly as a squirrel inched its way down the rope to the feeder. "Oh well, I guess I'll ask him about it tomorrow."

Josh sped down the road to his next stop.

The hardest part of this job is getting out of each house without being smothered to death, he thought. Of course, there were a few on his route who were too far gone to do much talking, and Mrs. Bennett was always curt and gave him the evil eye because of his hair. He could count on making up a little lost time with them, but with the rest he tried to say hello and leave before he was dragged into a conversation. He felt sorry for them, but if he spent just five extra minutes with each one, it added almost an hour to his route.

He took the turns on the winding road as fast as he could to make up for lost time and didn't see the nail-studded board in his lane until it was too late. There was a loud pop, and the wheel began to shake. He fought for control, fishtailing back and forth on the rough asphalt. The car slowed, and he pulled over onto the shoulder. Josh sat there for a minute, his hands shaking, then got out and walked around the car. On the far side he stopped, the flat tire grinning back at him. He gave it a solid kick and looked up at the sky for help.

"Why me?" he said aloud. Then, shaking his head, he opened the trunk and took out the jack and spare.

The sun was already going down when Josh finally made it to Mr. Davis's house. He opened the back door to find the old man sitting at the kitchen table, going through a box of old letters and photographs.

"You're late," Mr. Davis said, looking up over the top of his reading glasses at the clock on the wall. "For a minute there I thought I'd scared you off."

"It's been a rough day," Josh said, putting the dinner on the kitchen counter.

"What happened?" he asked.

"Well, to start with, Mrs. Howard's window wouldn't open."

"She caught you, eh?" he said with a sympathetic smile. "My, but that woman can talk. Once she gets you hooked, the only way out is to cut the line yourself."

"It turns out it was just locked," Josh said, rolling his eyes.

Mr. Davis chuckled. "She cornered me at the store once, and I thought I'd never get out alive."

"Then, I had a flat tire," he said, not finding any humor in the situation.

"A little exercise never hurt anyone," Mr. Davis quipped.

Josh had been trying to hold on to his dark mood in the face of the old man's banter but gave up. He pulled up a chair across from him and picked up one of the photographs on the table.

"What's all this?" he asked as he looked at a faded picture of a man standing in front of a long string of fish.

"Memories, son," Mr. Davis said, looking down at the box and then back at the boy. "I get these out from time to time so I won't forget."

"Is that you?" Josh asked, pointing to the man in the picture.

"No, that's my father," Mr. Davis said, glancing at the photograph. "He was quite a fisherman."

Josh examined the picture, then put it down and picked up an envelope from the pile. He turned it over in his hands, looking at the address and postmark.

"Before the telephone took over, people wrote letters," Mr. Davis said, nodding at the one Josh was holding. "It was really the only way to communicate except for telegrams, which were expensive and impersonal. But you could pour your heart out in a letter. It was something to hold on to, something you could get out and read again and again."

He took off his reading glasses and settled back in the chair.

"A phone call is gone as soon as you hang up," he continued. "But people always take the easy way out, so letters have become a thing of the past. It's a big mistake. Who's ever heard of the collected phone calls of Ernest Hemingway?"

"Well, now there's E-mail," Josh said.

"E-mail?"

"You know, letters sent by computer over the phone lines."

"Huhh. A push of a button and it's gone back to the ether it came from," Mr. Davis said skeptically.

"But you can print it out or save it on a disk if you want. We do it all the time at school."

"Can you put a drop of perfume on it before you seal it?"

"Well, no," Josh conceded.

"Can you send it on pale blue stationery that still holds a hint of lilacs after fifty years?" he said, holding up a letter from the pile in front of him.

"No. But it's a lot faster, and you can check the spelling and change things without having to cross them out."

"Can you see the handwriting, which tells so much about an individual's personality that there are experts who can describe you to a T without even reading the words?"

Josh opened his mouth to say something, but the old man didn't give him a chance.

"And those mistakes you mentioned, those Freudian slips that were overlooked and might tell you more than the whole rest of the letter. You would eliminate them, too?" he continued, just getting wound up. "And misspellings—man isn't perfect, you know. Would you take away his imperfection? His very humanity?"

"No," Josh said, a little confused. "I mean, I never really thought about it like that."

"I didn't think so," Mr. Davis said. "It's just not the same. Everything today has to be done in a hurry. Computers, telephones, jet planes, discount stores. What's the big rush? Where's the human factor? In my day things were slower. There weren't so many distractions. You had time to sit and reflect."

"But today you've *got* to hustle," Josh said.

"My mother has to work *and* fix these dinners just to make ends meet."

"We've always had to earn a living, Josh, it's more than that. If people bought less things, that they don't really need anyway, they wouldn't have to burn the candle at both ends to pay the bills. We're using up the earth's resources faster than we can blink, and all the while the things that matter the most are ignored."

"But it seems like wanting more has always been a problem," Josh countered. "That's what war is about, isn't it?"

"Sometimes. But what hurts is that so few people even try to see beyond the pale today. When I was growing up, we took turns reading aloud every night—*that* was our television. There was time to just sit on the porch and rock, there wasn't this compulsion to fill every quiet moment with activity. We felt comfortable with silence back then; now it seems to make people nervous. I didn't mean to get on a soapbox, Josh," he added apologetically. "I just feel that for all its glitter and technical marvels the world today is a much poorer place."

Mr. Davis paused for a moment and looked down at the table. "You asked me what I was doing with these?" he said, indicating the box in front of him.

Josh nodded.

"Besides what's up here," he said, tapping his forehead, "this is almost all I have left." He picked up some of the letters and thumbed through them. "Most of these are letters that my wife and I wrote to each other. Some of them go back to the days when we were courting, others are from when I was in the Second World War. They've been a great comfort to me." He opened one and looked at it. "Since Mary passed away I get them out from time to time and read them. Would you like to see them?"

"Sure," Josh answered, uncertain what else to say.

Mr. Davis put the letter he was holding back in the envelope and gathered up the others that were scattered on the table. He put them all back in the box and slid it across the table to Josh.

"Here," he said. "Take them home, read them, and copy the best ones down in your notebook. Don't change anything, just write them as they were written. Then, when you're through, bring them back to me."

"But how will I know which ones are the best ones?"

"You'll know. Just use your own judgment." He looked out the window at the darkening sky. "It's getting late," he said, standing up slowly. "You better get a move on or your mother will be worried."

Josh picked up the box and opened the door. "I'll take care of them," he said, indicating the box.

"You better," Mr. Davis told him.

*   *   *

Josh's mother looked up from the kitchen table when he opened the back door. The table was covered with bills, and she had been debating which ones to put off paying until the child support check arrived. She still had the name tag from the store pinned to her dress but had taken off her shoes to relieve her aching feet.

"What's in the box?" she asked.

"Old pictures and letters that Mr. Davis gave me to look at," he said, holding the box down low for her to see. "He wants me to copy some of them in the notebook."

"There are so many," she said, picking up an envelope and opening it. "This one is from Mary Wainwright to William Davis." She skimmed down the first page. "It's about a Mardi Gras ball he took her to in Mobile when they were dating."

A single flower petal fell from between the pages into her lap. She picked it up and held it in the palm of her hand.

"This must be from the corsage she wore," she said, gazing wistfully at the dried petal. She folded the letter with the petal inside and carefully put it back in the envelope.

"It seems Mr. Davis is trusting you with a lot, Josh. Try to hold them gently, they're very old and fragile."

"Yes, ma'am."

"It's late," she said, putting the letter back on top of the pile. "I'll fix you something to eat."

He carried the box down the hall to his room. When he opened the door, the bird chirped in its cage, hopping back and forth on the perch.

"Well, you look better," Josh said, putting down the box and walking over to the cage. "And you've been eating." The jar lid was empty, and hulls from the seeds littered the floor of the cage.

He changed the paper and filled the lid again with seed. "I'll have to see if I can catch you a cricket or worm," he said, rubbing the bird's chest with his finger.

Back in the kitchen, Josh sat down to the plate of tuna casserole his mother put in front of him. He had smelled it all afternoon in the car as he'd delivered the meals, and even though it was one of his favorites, the close quarters hadn't done much to help his appetite.

Josh looked at the clock by his bed and saw that it was after eleven. As he put down his schoolbook and leaned over to turn out the light, he noticed the box of letters still sitting on the floor. He reached down, took one off the top of the stack, and opened it.

November 10, 1943

Dear Mary,
    Not much has happened since I wrote you last. We've only flown one mission this week due to

bad weather. It's getting pretty cold here. There was ice in the cup of water one of the guys left outside last night, and it snowed on Monday. This is a little much for a southern boy to take! At least the clothes we've been issued are warm, though it's cold up in the plane anytime of year. I feel like a father to these young boys; in fact, they've started calling me "the old man."

I'm not supposed to talk about our missions, so I won't, except to say that in some ways I think my job is the hardest one on the plane. It's not bad most of the time—I'm busy with maps and coordinates and there's a lot going on, so that by the time we get sighted on the target and make the drop, I'm pretty worn out.

It's on the ride home that the trouble begins. My job is over, and all I have to do is wait. You would think that would be the easy part, but it's not. I sit and close my eyes and try to rest, but the noise of the engines and the flak make it impossible. So I try to concentrate on what's going on in the plane, but before I know it my mind begins to wander.

I think about the bombs we've just released, not knowing if they found their target or went wide of the mark. Then I start to wonder what might be wide of the mark. It could be a little house with a wife cooking dinner for her child while her husband is off fighting. I know this is a just war, or at least as close to it as war can be. I know that I have it easy compared to the guys on the ground doing the dirty work, but it's the waiting and thinking that are the worst part.

We've got some fellows here that don't seem to give what we're doing a second thought, then there are others that take it a lot harder than I do. I worry about what will happen to you and my little boy if I don't

The letter stopped abruptly and wasn't signed. Josh turned over the tattered envelope and noticed that it had never been post-marked. As he was putting it back in the box, his eye caught another envelope with the same date postmarked on the outside. When he opened it, a faded black-and-white photograph fell out. He picked it up and saw a group of men standing by the nose of a bomber. A large tarpon jumping out of the water was painted on its side, with "Silver King" written in flowing script underneath. He put down the picture and read the letter with it:

November 10, 1943

Dear Mary,

Well, we've had it easy this week. The weather has kept us grounded every day but one, and that trip was a piece of cake. George left a cup of water outside last night and it froze solid, so it's getting kind of chilly here! Good thing we've got lots of warm clothes and blankets!

Due to the weather we've mostly stayed in the barracks playing cards or reading. Jamie got a natural royal flush in poker yesterday! The first time I've ever seen that happen. He had such a surprised look on his face that everyone bailed out on him the minute he raised the stakes. It made him furious, but we got a laugh out of it. A good player would have thrown his cards in and left them guessing, but not our Jamie. He wasn't happy until he had shown everyone in the barracks what he had!

Thanks for the candy and books you sent, I just got them yesterday. I'm reading the mystery now. Lots of creaking doors and screams in the night, hope it doesn't keep me up! I've been sleeping like a baby and putting on weight from all the easy living here. I'm enclosing a picture of me and the boys standing by our plane. Sorry it's not very good of me. I guess I'm just not that photogenic.

Give my love to Mother and Dad. I'm glad you're going over the bay for Thanksgiving. Give my beautiful boy a big kiss from his father! It's time for lights out, so I'll write again soon.

Much Love,
Will

Josh looked at the photograph again and by process of elimination recognized Mr. Davis. He look tired and thin, but his eyes were unchanged. He put the letter back in the box and turned out the light, lying on his back in the dark and staring at the ceiling.

He could almost hear the roar of the big

engines and the thud of flak against the side of the plane. He remembered the film they had watched in history on the war, and the footage of bombing missions. But the tiny houses and factories on the screen had always seemed like toys as the puffs of smoke showed where the bombs hit.

He rolled over on his side and closed his eyes, but sleep wasn't soon in coming.

Chapter 7

Blinded by the Light

As the sun rose over the horizon, a stray beam of light found its way through an opening in the curtain and crawled slowly over the bed to shine in Josh's eyes. He stirred and tried to burrow deeper in the covers, but the light was unrelenting. Finally he rolled over as the beam continued around the room. It illuminated the posters of rock stars and surfers that covered the walls, then moved slowly past the birdcage, over a stack of schoolbooks, and across the box of letters on the floor. It seemed to linger on the surfboard leaning against the wall in the corner, tracing the curve of the delicately arched fin.

The ray of light came to a mirror partly obscured by snapshots forced into the gap between wood and glass: Josh's mother and father, frozen forever in laughter; he and his two friends from school, standing arm in arm; and a photo of Josh surfing last summer, intent upon the wave and oblivious of the camera. Here in the mirror, the beam was magnified by the thin coating of silver spread on glass and deflected back at the sleeping boy.

Josh opened his eyes and squinted into the glare. Sitting up, he stretched and then drew back the curtain on the window and let the morning light flood the room. He noted the blue sky and the light breeze warming the air and knew it would be a perfect day. The first good weekend of the year for surfing.

He took a long shower, then dressed in jeans and a sweatshirt before padding barefoot down the hall to the kitchen. Over a bowl of cereal he sat looking at the morning paper. All very bleak stuff: a girl abducted in Atlanta as she walked home from school, another new horror tale from some distant war in a country he hadn't even known existed, and a reluctant recall of cars with faulty brakes after twenty-four people had been killed.

After breakfast he made a peanut-butter-and-jelly sandwich. He put it in a plastic bag and stuffed it into a side pocket of his pack—which already bulged with a wet suit, surfboard wax, and a towel. The sun was high in the sky by the time he finished loading his board on the Volkswagen and backed down the driveway.

It was a thirty-mile drive to the jetty, and

he drove it at a slow cruising speed with the windows rolled down and the radio turned up. The cheerful island sounds of Jimmy Buffett filled the car, and Josh remembered the book of short stories he had read. He took a deserted back road to the beach so he wouldn't have to drive by the miles of condos and stores that had sprung up in the past few years. The water was getting close now, and without realizing it, he increased his speed.

He emerged into the harsh light of the beach and turned in the parking lot at the jetty. There were four other cars there besides his own, split evenly between surfers and fishermen. An uneasy truce existed between the two groups, and hostilities had been known to run high. The best surfing and fishing spots often overlapped, and each side claimed them as their own.

He unstrapped his board, slung his pack over one shoulder, and hiked across the dunes that separated the parking lot from the beach. The sea oats swayed in the breeze, and the sand was warm on his bare feet. The long walk made this beach unpopular with tourists, and for that reason alone it was his favorite spot. He could tell from the cars in the parking lot that Chris and Mark would be the only other ones out today.

Josh crested the last dune and looked down the wide beach to the water beyond. This first look at the waves was one of the moments he liked best. Sure, the radio had given a surf report this morning saying the seas were running at two to four feet with a five- to ten-mile-an-hour northerly breeze. But to a surfer that was about as informative as describing van Gogh as the guy who used lots of paint. To a surfer every day was different, and in the fickle shore break of the Gulf of Mexico the conditions often changed radically from morning to afternoon.

He stood for a few minutes on the peak of the dune, watching the scene unfold below. The winter storms had shifted the sandbar, and he would have to find the best breaks all over again. The long rock jetty—brought down boulder by boulder on barges from Birmingham—lay to the east, marking one side of the channel. It broke the otherwise monotonous stretch of beach, causing the prevailing westerly current to form an eddy behind it. Sand piled up and formed bars at an angle to the beach, which was what made surfing the jetty different from surfing the rest of the Alabama coast.

As he watched, Mark caught a wave. He was quickly up on his board, turning to his left. He made a sharp turn at the top, plunging back down and then digging his rail in hard and cutting back to go airborne over the crest of the crashing wave. Josh could just hear his whoop of triumph above the noise of the surf. Following Mark's progress from his spot past the breakers, Chris spied Josh standing alone on the top of the dune and waved. Josh waved back and jogged the rest of the way down to the beach.

He dropped his pack and board on the hard sand by the water's edge and sat there for a few minutes, sizing up the waves. It was a ritual he never varied: get the big picture from the top of the dune, then sit on the beach, watching the waves to see how they were breaking and getting a feel for the day.

Waves are born of the wind; they are the wind made visible. Far out in the gulf the wind blows, and gradually the ripples it produces coalesce into swells. All of this is fed by the wind; it shapes and molds the water like a sculptor molding clay. This nebulous beginning leads to the inevitable constant in surfing that no two days are ever alike.

Having seen enough, Josh put on his shorty, a wet suit that covered his chest and upper legs like a tank top and shorts. Even though the air was warm, the water still held the chill of winter. He knelt beside his board and rubbed the stick of wax over the top surface to give him better traction on the slick fiberglass. Then he attached the ankle strap around his leg and, gritting his teeth against the cold, waded out into the water.

When the water reached his waist, he pulled himself prone on the board and began to paddle out. The bottom dropped away beneath him as he propelled himself forward. He worked his way through the swirling currents and chop until the color of the water lightened abruptly, then he hopped off onto the shallow sandbar.

He had arrived just as a set was coming in

and watched as Chris and Mark took back-to-back waves. Mark was the more radical surfer of the two, making sharp cutbacks and taking risks that Chris and Josh would have avoided. He always pushed himself to the limit, not content unless he had dominated the wave. Chris was more tentative, making few turns and just satisfied with a long ride. He was more a surfer by association than occupation—he lived near the beach and his friends were surfers, so he was, too.

Their individual styles mirrored their personalities out of the water. Mark, with his dark features and stocky athletic build, was the fiery rebel always one step away from disaster. He had been suspended in the fall for getting in a fight with a football player at school. It was a bloody fight, most of it being Mark's. Were he to be asked what it had been about, he probably wouldn't be able to remember except that the guy had made some remark that rubbed him the wrong way. He was quick with his temper, but just as quick to laugh. He attracted girls like a magnet and always knew the right thing to say to keep them interested.

Chris was a follower. He always did everything one step behind Mark and Josh. His sandy hair and freckled face held nothing but an earnest desire to be liked, to come along for the ride. He went out of his way to avoid trouble, but if Mark stuck his foot in it, Chris would be right behind him.

It had been the three of them against the

world for as long as Josh could remember. They even referred to themselves as the Three Musketeers.

Their waves spent, Chris and Mark waded over to him, and they all paddled out together.

"Did you see me rebound off the lip?" Mark asked rhetorically. "I really ripped it!"

"It was okay," Josh replied blandly.

"Okay? Let's see you try that one!" Mark shot back.

"At least you didn't break your arm this time," Chris said, razzing him.

"How was I supposed to know it was only a foot deep?"

"I don't know, maybe you could have looked first?" Josh responded with a smile. Mark's arm cocked back and swept around in his direction, sending a shower of spray over Josh as he paddled away, laughing.

When they were outside the breakers, they stopped paddling and sat back on their boards. Now that Josh was used to it, the water had lost its sting and felt only cool and refreshing. He leaned back as far as he could and dipped his hair in it. Then, rotating his dangling legs, he turned his board and paddled farther out than the others, hoping for a big set. As he stopped paddling and sat back up, he saw the humped peak of a rogue wave coming in fast.

Mark and Chris saw it, too, and started paddling out, just managing to make it over the rising face before it started to break. Josh was already up when he passed them, and the only sound was the hiss of his board through the water as he picked up speed on the unbroken face. He carved broad, sweeping turns with a grace and beauty that were missing from Mark's flashy style.

A gust of northerly wind caused the wave to steepen and hollow. Josh turned at the bottom and leveled off as a tube started to form. Sensing it, he adjusted his weight and angle to slow his forward progress slightly. As the wave began to gain on him, he bent his knees. When it was right behind him, he bent his back to lower his profile still further. Then it was all around him, and he crouched down fully, holding the rail with one hand to steady himself. He extended his other hand toward the smooth face of the wave, letting his fingers skim along its gossamer surface to caress it gently. Feeling that a balance had been reached that could not be sustained, he pressed harder on the rail and shot out the end of the tube as it collapsed behind him with a blast of air.

The wave died, and he was propelled off the end of the bar into deeper water. His forward motion slowed, and he dropped prone on the board, heading back out. He paddled steadily, his arms flashing in the sun. The sea stretched farther than he could ever imagine, and as he took in the vastness that surrounded him, he felt whole and complete.

Josh sensed something and felt a prickle on the back of his neck. Turning, he looked over his shoulder and saw the sun shining down on him. He closed his eyes, forgetting everything else, and was filled with its warmth and light.

Chapter 8

_____ ⟨ఌ⟩ _____

Red Sky at Morning

Mr. Davis awoke before the sun. His arthritis was acting up again, but he knew it was more than that. Lately he had felt a restlessness deep inside him that wouldn't leave him alone. Maybe it was spring tugging at long buried instincts, maybe it was bringing up all these old memories with the boy, or maybe it was just the thought of being old and realizing that he didn't have much time left.

The pain was always worse in the morning, and he grimaced as he moved his stiff joints. He dressed slowly, concentrating on every button, then shuffled down the hall to the kitchen. He plugged in the coffeepot and set about making himself breakfast. He hadn't had much of an appetite lately but went through the motions anyway. Soon the coffee was perking, and the smell of bacon frying filled the air. He cooked two eggs, made some toast, and sat at the kitchen table to eat. Breakfast had always been his favorite meal, and even without much of an appetite it still tasted good.

The house around him was quiet. Only the ticking of the mantel clock and the clink of silverware against china were audible. In the silence, time seemed insubstantial. He closed his eyes and felt the years slip away.

He saw Mary standing at the stove, her profile backlit by the early morning light. He saw every detail of her: the nose that turned up slightly at the end, her graying auburn hair pinned loosely back, the way her lips parted slightly as she concentrated on the bacon in the pan, and blue eyes that could freeze water or melt ice.

"What a beautiful day!" she said, looking out the window. "Spring is my favorite time of year. Let's work on the flower garden again today."

"I think any time of year is your favorite," he said with a smile from the kitchen table. "It doesn't seem to matter if it's pouring down rain or the sky is as blue as a robin's egg."

"Look!" she said, pointing. "The bulbs are finally starting to bloom."

He got up from the table and came to stand behind her at the window, putting his hands around her waist and breathing in deeply.

"I'm so glad you convinced me to move back here, Will," she said, reaching up to take his hand.

"What I like is watching it change," he said, nodding to the water just visible around the corner of the house. "Today the bay is as calm as a lake, but by tomorrow a storm might blow in and it could look like a pot that's about to boil over. It's constantly in motion, constantly changing."

"You've always had a way with words, Will Davis," she said, looking over her shoulder at him. "I guess that's why I married you."

He opened his eyes and looked down at his half-empty plate of cold eggs then over to the now vacant stove. His ears rang with distant voices just out of range, and the air before him shimmered like a mirage. He reached for his heart medicine and put a pill in his mouth, waiting for it to take effect. He felt so fragile lately. It's probably just the time of year, he thought. As soon as summer gets here, I'll be fine again. The ringing slowly subsided, and his vision started to clear.

He pushed his chair back from the table and put the dishes in the sink. Moving listlessly through the rooms, he found himself on the porch and sat down in his rocker, looking out over the bay. Everything still looks the same, he thought, but it's empty now.

He sat there for a long while, watching the day begin. First, the sounds of birds heralding the dawn. Then, the red glow behind the trees, lighting up the sky. Finally, the sun itself, peeking over the horizon to tint the water.

"Red sky at morning, sailors take warning," he said, speaking the worn old adage before he even realized he was thinking it.

A breeze began to blow off the water toward him, breaking the glassy surface into infinite reflections of the rising sun. Sometimes his eyes closely examined the world around him, while at other times they appeared glazed as he sank into his own inner world.

He felt a tear forming in the corner of his eye. It must be the glare off the water, he thought as he wiped it away with the back of his hand.

Chapter 9

A Missing Piece

Josh closed the door to his room and picked up the notebook and a handful of letters from the box on the floor. The bird cocked his head and watched as Josh arranged the pillows behind him, then lay back on the bed and opened the first envelope. Each night he had managed to read a few of them, and gradually the old man's life was coming into clearer focus. He looked over at the box of letters, which reminded him of pieces of a puzzle.

Josh remembered when he and his mother had worked on a jigsaw puzzle together. He had been eleven at the time and had been in bed with the flu for almost a week. Even the novelty of television had finally worn off, and the endless daytime reruns began to run together until it was hard to tell one from another.

His mother sat on the edge of his bed, putting her hand on his forehead. She looked at her watch and removed the thermometer from his mouth.

"You still have a little fever, but it's going down," she said, smoothing back his matted hair. "Do you feel like getting up?"

He managed a cough and nodded solemnly.

"Good. I'll see if I can find a game for us to play."

She kissed the top of his head and left the room. He heard her pull down the steps to the attic, and in a minute she returned carrying a box.

"I found this," she said, holding the jigsaw puzzle for him to see. "But the picture on the lid is missing, so I'm not sure what it's supposed to be."

"I guess it'll be a surprise," he said.

"More like a miracle, you mean, if we can put it together without it," she answered.

They cleared off the kitchen table and arranged the pieces face up on it. It seemed as if there were thousands of them. He separated the edges from the rest, while his mother tried to make some sense of the subtle shades of blue and green.

"Chris called," Josh said as he fit two pieces together.

"How did he say school was going?" she asked.

"Pretty boring, except that Tommy Barlow threw up all over his desk yesterday."

"Poor Miss Montgomery," she said, shaking her head sympathetically.

"Chris said that for a minute it looked like she was going to join him," Josh said with a grin, forgetting that he was sick.

"I'm surprised she's still here," she replied. "I took one look at her when school started and wondered if she would last till Christmas."

"I wasn't sure she would, either, after someone put a snake in her desk," he said, attaching a corner to the string of pieces he had joined.

"Why do I get the feeling that Mark had something to do with that," she said, watching him out of the corner of her eye for a reaction.

Josh flinched. "Are you sure you don't have any more edge pieces over there?" he asked, ignoring her question.

"I don't see any."

"Well, we must be missing a piece, then," he said in frustration.

"Keep looking," she replied. "It's probably right in front of you."

"Dad's going to take me fishing again when he comes back," he said, matter-of-factly.

It was her turn to flinch. She put down the piece she was holding and looked at him.

"Last time we caught a speckled trout and a flounder," he said, continuing to search for the missing piece. "I caught the flounder," he added proudly.

"Josh—"

"Next time we're gonna rent a boat instead of going out on the pier. You catch more from a boat," he said, mimicking his father's words. He picked up a piece and tried it, and it fit perfectly. "You were right," he said, glancing up at her with a smile before returning to the puzzle.

"Josh," she repeated, putting her hand on top of his, "listen to me."

He dragged his eyes reluctantly away from the puzzle and looked at her. He didn't like what he saw and tried to turn away, but her eyes wouldn't let him go.

"I got a call today." She paused. "I've been trying to think how to tell you," she said, and faltered.

He knew from her tone of voice that it was something he didn't want to hear. He opened his mouth to fill the void, but she beat him to it.

"He's not coming back," she said as gently as possible.

Josh looked down at the unread letter in his hand. They had never finished the puzzle, and for the first time it occurred to him to try to picture what it might have been. He closed his eyes and tried to assemble the shadowy outline and blur of colors into something meaningful. Could you leave out some of the pieces and still see the picture? he wondered. But maybe it's the other way around. *Maybe the whole picture is contained in each separate piece.*

He concentrated on the letter in his hand, reading it through twice. Then he opened the notebook to a blank page and began to copy it down.

Chapter 10

Heartwood

Josh arrived at Mr. Davis's house early on Friday afternoon, his deliveries going quickly for a change. He had finished reading the box of letters and brought them with him to return. They sat in the rockers on the porch and talked.

"A lot of my family history is tied up in this place," Mr. Davis began. "My grandfather came here in 1870. He was tired of struggling to make ends meet in Mobile after the war, so he loaded up everything he had—including his young bride—and set out across the bay."

Josh wrote as fast as he could in the notebook, trying to keep up without interrupting.

"He took a boat to the Eastern Shore and opened a general store with money he had inherited from his father. They lived in a room above it for a few years until the business got off the ground, then he started looking around for somewhere to build. One day he rode his horse along the road that followed the bay and found this piece of land." He looked around him at the big oaks draped with Spanish moss.

"I like to think of him forcing his way through the underbrush until he came out here. I can see him looking out over the bay from this spot for the first time." The old man had a distant look in his eyes as he gazed out over the water.

"Maybe it was in the spring, on a day just like today. The world was still new here then, nothing in sight for as far as the eye could see. Now it's wall-to-wall houses from here to Fairhope, but then it was desolate. It was a bold move to pick a spot overlooking the water—what with storms that blew in without warning. I like to think he did it because he loved the bay, but my father never talked about him very much. He died before I was born, so all I can do is speculate. Would you like to see a picture of him?"

"Sure," Josh said, putting down his pen.

Mr. Davis went inside and returned with a faded sepia photograph that he handed to Josh. It was of a middle-aged man with penetrating eyes, his dark hair swept back off his forehead. He was dressed in a suit and wore a very serious expression. But upon closer examination, Josh thought he could detect the trace of a smile in the corners of his mouth.

"He built this house himself in his spare time. It took him nearly two years. After they moved in he bought a horse and buggy and taught my grandmother how to drive it so she could come into town whenever she wanted. He used to ride his horse to work at the store every day except Sundays and holidays."

"I can't imagine riding a horse all the way to town every day," Josh said as he handed the picture back to him.

"In bad weather it would be a problem all

right," Mr. Davis agreed. "My father was born in this house, and as my grandfather grew older he hired someone to run the store and started spending more time out here. He was an avid fisherman and built the first wharf out front there."

"That's where the board you showed me came from," Josh said, remembering their discussion on the pier.

"Correct."

"He built this house by himself?"

"Pretty much. A couple of workers from the store helped him with it. They cut the big beams from cypress trees not far from here and squared them up by hand with an ax and adze. The rest of the lumber was cut at a sawmill in town, and the millwork was made in Mobile and shipped over by boat."

"It looks like it's still in good shape," Josh said, examining the house.

"It's held up well, considering all it's gone through," he said. "This old-growth cypress was a beautiful wood to work with and stands up to the elements better than anything else around. Too bad it's all gone now."

"But I saw some cypress fencing for sale at the discount store just the other day," Josh told him.

"It might be the same species," he said, "but that doesn't make it the same wood. Most cypress today is cut from small, fast-growing trees. It's not like the virgin timber that was here back then. Those trees grew slowly, shaded by other large trees when they were young. And since no one was here to cut them, they lived to a ripe old age. Long slow growth meant dense wood that's strong and heavy. It also meant more heartwood, and to resist the elements a board has to be all heartwood."

"Heartwood?" Josh said, looking up.

"As a tree grows, the wood near the center slowly changes to heartwood. It takes on color, absorbing minerals from the soil as it draws water up through its roots. It's the only part of the tree that's truly resistant to decay."

The old man nodded his head in respect as he looked at the house. "He designed it himself, you know."

"You mean without an architect?" Josh asked, amazed.

"That's right. It was common back then, the Renaissance man's approach to life. There were books that were used to get the basic proportions right, then you filled in the details on your own. Just a minute and I'll show you what I mean."

He went inside and returned with an old book, which he handed to the boy.

"This belonged to my grandfather."

Josh opened it to the first yellowed page and read the title: *The American Builder's Companion* by Asher Benjamin. He thumbed through it and saw notes written in the margins. On a blank page at the back there was even a pen-and-ink drawing of the front of the house where they were sitting.

"If you followed the basic rules of scale and proportion, then everything else fell into place. Of course, my grandfather didn't have to worry with plumbers, electricians, or building inspectors, so I guess in many ways building was a lot simpler back then. But you couldn't just run down to the local building supply and drive home with a truck full of lumber, so maybe in the long run it balances out."

"I don't think I could do it if I had a dozen books," Josh said as he handed it back to Mr. Davis.

"Have you ever built anything?" he said, looking over at the boy.

"Not really," Josh replied. "Unless you count a tree house in the backyard when I was little."

"I guess I built my share of those, too. It's hard not to with all the good climbing trees around here," he said with a smile. "When you build something, it's like turning your dreams into reality. You can see it, touch it, and know it will be there long after you're gone. It's a good feeling. Of course it takes a lot of practice and some natural ability, too."

He leaned forward in his rocker and rested his elbows on the arms. "When I was a boy, I spent a summer working for an old cabinetmaker. I had just turned fourteen, and it was my first summer job. He wasn't exactly an easy man to work for. I had to be there early, so I would ride into town with my father every morning on his way to the store...."

"Will," his father said, leaning over the bed and shaking the boy gently. "It's time to get up, son."

Will sat up and forced his eyes open in the dark room. His father lit the kerosene lamp by his bed and left. Will's eyes closed slowly and his head lolled back until it hit the headboard of the bed with a dull thump. He opened them again, swung his legs over the side of the bed, and sat there for a minute, rubbing the sleep out of his eyes.

After he had dressed, he went down to the kitchen. His mother was busy at the stove, and his father was just finishing his coffee. He sat at the table, and his mother brought him his breakfast.

"Looks like it'll be another hot one," his father commented. "What's Mr. Jones got you doing these days?"

"Oh, the usual," Will said, a note of boredom creeping into his voice, "cleaning up, getting him wood, running errands."

"It takes a long time to learn a trade like cabinetmaking, and Mr. Jones has been at it for as long as I can remember. Try to watch what he's doing, you might learn something."

"I have, but I thought he would let me make something, not just sweep up."

"He didn't hire you to teach you his business. He hired you to do the heavy lifting and the things he doesn't have time to do. He's getting old, you know, and with his back I'm amazed he's still working at all."

Mr. Jones was hard to get along with, and Will never seemed to be able to please him. After two months on the job, the boy no longer looked forward to getting up in the morning. In fact, he had begun to wonder if he would last the summer. He couldn't quit—not with his father getting him the job—but he could get fired whether he wanted to or not, and lately the old man seemed close to giving him the ax.

He seemed to expect Will to know what to do without ever explaining it to him, and if he didn't do it just right the first time, he blessed him out. But if the boy questioned him about something, the old man gave him hell just for asking. It was a lose-lose situation. Will tried to stay out of his way, keeping a broom in his hand and trying to look busy, but that seldom worked.

After breakfast he helped his father crank the Ford, and they headed for town. It was full light by the time he dropped Will off at the shop, and Mr. Jones was already busy working at his bench. Without looking up, he gave the boy his chores for the morning.

"You can start by bringing me a good cherry one-by-twelve from the shed, then clean up that mess on the floor over there."

"Yes, sir."

Will walked out to the lumber shed that was attached to the main building. At least this time he knew where the stack of cherry was. The last time he'd looked for half an hour before timidly asking the old man, which had brought on an explosion about what the younger generation was coming to today. Will dug through the pile, found a piece twelve inches wide, and brought it back to the shop. Mr. Jones barely glanced at the board.

"You call that a *good* piece? Why, I could get a dog to drag in the first board he came to! Now take it back out there and bring me something I can use, something without all those knots in it."

"Yes, sir."

Will returned the rejected piece to the shed and began pulling out all the wide boards from the stack. He lined them all up against the side of the shed and examined them carefully, then picked out the best one of the bunch. He carried it back to the shop and began cleaning up.

As he swept, Will watched the old man. He was bent over his bench, working on a front door for the new bakery in town. Yesterday Will had helped him assemble it, knocking the mortise-and-tenon frame together with a mallet. Then Mr. Jones had driven in the tapered pegs that locked the joints in place while the boy held it for him. Now, Will watched him plane the surfaces smooth.

The morning light filtered through the dusty glass of the shop windows, causing the cypress to shimmer as the old man pushed the sharp hand plane across the door's surface. Paper-thin curls of shavings issued from the top of the plane and drifted down as gently as a feather to the floor under his feet. Mr. Jones concentrated on the wood before him, seemingly oblivious of the boy. The plane made a soothing swish as it passed over the wood, and he paused from time to time to rub his hand over the smooth surface. Satisfied with the result, he called Will to help him turn the door over to plane the other side.

As Will helped him lift the heavy door, the old man grunted in pain. They set it down, and he held his back with one hand while he gripped the bench tightly with the other to steady himself. After the worst had passed, he looked at Will.

"Boy, why don't you finish up this side for me."

"Me?"

"That's what I said, didn't I?"

Will picked up the plane from the bench and tentatively pushed it across the long stile of the door. Immediately it dug into the wood, tearing a small gouge in the surface. The old man sighed and took it from his hand.

"First of all, you have to be going in the right direction," he said, pointing to the edge of the door. "See how the grain runs out at an angle to the surface? You have to plane with it, not against it. It's kind of like brushing a horse. You wouldn't brush him from back to front, would you?"

"No, sir," Will replied meekly.

"Second, you have to put some muscle into it, long hard strokes with some weight behind them. Third, take a shallow pass. Feel the blade with your thumb to see how deep it's cutting."

He showed Will how to adjust the plane and backed the blade out a little, then had him feel it again.

"See, it won't cut as deep now. Try it again."

Will faced the other direction, braced his legs, and pushed hard against the door. The plane slid forward smoothly, and he extended his arms, shifting his weight with the stroke as a shaving curled up from the throat.

"That's better. Now level out the joint where the rail meets the stile so they're flush."

Will worked the plane along the spot where the two pieces joined, taking the high one down while trying not to dig into the other board.

The old man moved stiffly over to his stool and watched the boy work, not taking his eyes off him for a moment. Will continued to plane the door, carefully leveling and smoothing the wood. Mr. Jones watched until he was sure the boy knew what he was doing.

"I'm going inside for a little while. Clean up that mess when you're through and sweep up the rest of the shop. I'll be back soon."

Will watched him hobble into the little house that adjoined the shop. Through the window he saw him sit down painfully on the sofa, then stretch out. He had never been left to do a job by himself before. He wasn't sure if it was because the old man had more confidence in him now or if his back had given him no choice. Regardless, he worked carefully, trying to do the best that he could. When he was through, he swept up the shavings around the bench.

As he was cleaning up, Mr. Jones walked back into the shop. He examined the door and without a word of praise called Will over to help him move it to the finishing room.

Mr. Jones went over to the shelves lined with numerous bottles and cans. He got several down and measured their contents in a cup, mixing the ingredients together in a quart can. Then he took a brush, dipped it in the can, and began to apply a full coat of the varnish. After a few minutes he noticed Will still standing there.

"What are you gawking at, boy? Surely you aren't through cleaning up?"

"Yes, sir. I am."

"Then go find a good cherry one-by-six and rip me off a ten-foot piece of two-by-two from that thick cherry board that's in the shed. And don't let me catch you dawdling out there like I did yesterday."

"Yes, sir," he said, leaving the room.

Will struggled to get the heavy cherry board onto a pair of sawhorses, then took the saw and, starting at one end, began the laborious process of ripping the narrow piece free from the larger board. Even with the shade from the big oak, the midday heat was intense. By the time his last stroke separated the two, his shirt was soaked and drops of sweat littered the board. He sat back, out of breath, his right arm hanging limp at his side. Flexing his hand, he noticed a large blister forming on his thumb and another one on his palm.

Mr. Jones stuck his head out the door and saw Will sitting there.

"Boy, don't make me dock your wages," he said, then disappeared back inside.

Will struggled to his feet, gathered up the saw and wood, and trudged into the shop.

"Put it over there by the other workbench," he said. "It's time for lunch."

Will picked up his lunch sack and followed Mr. Jones into the house. They ate at the table in silence while Will looked around at the carefully made cabinets and furniture that lined the walls. After lunch they left the relative cool of the house and walked back to the shop.

"You've been helping me for a while now," the old man said, "and it's time to see if you've learned anything. I have an order for a little bedside table in cherry. Here's what it should look like." He picked up a scrap of wood and made a quick sketch on it.

"Nothing fancy, just a plain top, tapered legs, and a drawer in the front apron." He penciled in some dimensions and handed the drawing to Will. "Square the wood up and cut it to length, and I'll help you get started."

"Yes, sir."

Will took the sketch and walked slowly over to the other bench where the pile of cherry awaited him. He didn't know quite what to make of this sudden trust that was being put in him. Was it a trap? Just one more way to show him how little he really knew?

He worked on the table the rest of the afternoon, planing the wood smooth and squaring up the edges. Mr. Jones showed him how to use the long jointer plane to straighten out a warped board and how to use a shooting board to square up the edges. When his father pulled up and honked for him, he found that for the first time he really didn't want to leave.

When he arrived the next morning, Mr. Jones had a list of errands for him to run in town, then he had to pull some lumber from the shed for his next project. It was well after lunch before he could finally get back to working on the table.

The old man came over and showed him how to lay out the mortises on the legs with a marking gauge, then he watched as the boy chiseled out the waste. Cutting the mortises was hard work, and Will took his time, being careful not to split the legs.

Little by little over the following weeks he made progress on the table. He had to take care of Mr. Jones's chores first, but he always found some time every day to devote to it. After the mortises were cut, Mr. Jones showed Will how to cut the tenons on the aprons to complete the joint. Will sawed carefully to the lines left by the marking gauge and was rewarded with a good fit when he finally slid the two parts together. After he had tapered the legs, the old man helped him assemble the table and peg the joints.

All that was left now was to make the drawer. Mr. Jones showed him how to lay out and cut the complicated dovetail joints and had him practice on scrap wood for several days until he got the hang of it. It took a fine saw, a keen eye, and a steady hand to cut exactly to the scribed lines. Finally the day came when he had cut the last of the joints. He tapped the pieces together with a block of wood and a mallet, and they meshed tightly. He felt someone behind him and turned to see the old man looking over his shoulder.

"There's a gap in that back corner," he said as he turned and shuffled back to his bench.

The summer was at an end, and so was the table. The new cherry gleamed under the coats of varnish Will had applied. As he looked at it, pride welled up inside of him. He had taken rough wood and turned it into something beautiful to behold.

He felt the old man behind him again.

"All through, are you? Let's have a look," Mr. Jones said and bent over to examine the table.

Sliding out the drawer, he checked the fit and noticed that it moved smoothly on the runners. He ran his hand over the top and turned to the boy.

"Not bad for a first try," he said.

Will beamed at the minor compliment, the first he had been offered since he had started working in the shop.

"Now don't go getting cocky on me, boy," Mr. Jones said, giving him a stern look.

Will's last week in the shop passed slowly. He returned to his regular chores, which seemed even more menial than before. The old man was working on a new display counter for the drugstore, and Will helped him fit the sliding doors and finish it.

On Friday Mr. Jones paid him for his last week of work and looked him in the eye as he handed him the money.

"You've got a job here next summer if you want it," he said.

"Thank you, sir," Will answered.

His father pulled up out front and honked. Mr. Jones held out his hand, and Will shook it, then he turned and walked quickly to the Ford. He looked back before they rounded the bend in the road and saw the old man disappear into the shop.

On the ride home, Will was lost in thought. He imagined Mr. Jones working alone in his shop, trying to bend over to clean up the floor or struggling to get a board off the rack.

After supper Will walked slowly up the stairs to his room. When he opened the door, he stopped motionless in the doorway. There, sitting in the middle of the floor, was his table. No card, no note, just the table. He walked up to it, running his hand over the smooth top, and smiled. He could almost feel the old man behind him again, looking over his shoulder.

"I still have that table," Mr. Davis said to Josh. "The cherry is dark with age now, and there's a crack in the top that developed one unusually cold winter. Other than that, it's held up well over the years. I guess it's almost an antique now, just like me."

"Did you ever work for him again?" Josh asked.

"I stopped by a couple of times after school that fall and helped out, but the subject of the table never came up. His back got worse that winter, until finally he had to close up the shop. In the spring his son came and took him to live with him in Mobile. We never heard from him again."

Josh closed the notebook and got up to leave.

"Are you busy tomorrow?" Mr. Davis asked.

Josh thought for a minute. "I don't think so," he said.

"I've got something I want to do, and I need your help. Are you interested?"

"Sure."

"Good. I'll see you in the morning, then."

Chapter 11

Song of the Wind

Josh opened the back door the next morning and found Mr. Davis busy at the kitchen counter. A picnic basket lay open on the table, and the room looked as though someone had ransacked the place. Hard-boiled eggs cooled in a bowl of water, while jars of home-made pickles and various condiments were strewn across the counter. The old man looked up from the ham he was carving.

"Come in, son, and make yourself useful," he said, nodding to the empty spot beside him.

Josh dropped the notebook on the table and set to work spreading mayonnaise and mustard on slices of homemade bread as Mr. Davis cut them off the loaf. The room was filled with the pungent aroma of baking.

"I made the bread myself this morning," he said, cutting another slice. "First time in years." His knife slowed its sawing motion. "There's something about the smell of bread baking. It smells like the earth itself. Maybe it comes from somewhere deep inside our collective unconscious, passed down through thousands of years like an extra chromosome."

"Collective unconscious?" Josh asked, looking at him out of the corner of his eye.

"Archetypes that are hardwired into our brain," the old man said as he began cutting another slice off the loaf.

"What?" Josh said.

Mr. Davis glanced over at him. "Ever heard of Jung?"

"No."

"Carl Jung was a Swiss psychologist. He spent years studying human behavior and became convinced that many of the things we think and do aren't learned in the traditional sense of the word. The more he observed, the more he came to believe that we're not just a blank sheet of paper waiting to be written on when we're born," the old man said, stacking the slices neatly to one side. "Jung decided that each of us comes into the world with knowledge already buried deep in our unconscious mind. Information that's handed down genetically rather than learned."

"Like instincts are in other animals?" Josh asked.

"Exactly. He called this knowledge archetypes. He thought that in addition to the memory each of us has of things that happen during our life, we also have a collective memory that goes back to the dawn of mankind and helps define what it means to be human."

"Everybody?" Josh asked.

"Everybody."

"All over the world?" Josh questioned, still not convinced.

"Yes."

"But people are so different. How could we

all share the same memory?" he asked, putting down his knife and layering on the ham.

"Many of our differences are really only superficial, Josh. Religion, for example, was one of Jung's favorite archetypes. Every culture we know of, now and in the distant past, has practiced some form of it. He felt that this didn't happen just by chance but was proof of a basic need we all share."

"But if I met a bushman from Africa, we wouldn't be anything alike," Josh said.

"You'd have more in common than you think."

"Like what?" Josh asked skeptically.

"Well, you would both have the same basic needs and feelings," Mr. Davis answered. "He'd feel love for his family, just like you do, and you both would look at a sunset with a sense of wonder."

"But we wouldn't even speak the same language, we wouldn't be able to communicate."

"Language isn't communication, son, it's just a *means* of communication. The older I get, the more I tend to see what we all have in common, rather than our differences. They're two sides of the same coin, you know. When I look at ancient art or read the literature of other times and places, what strikes me most is that they make so much sense. You would think there would be such a gulf between us that they wouldn't even be comprehensible. But not only do they make sense, they often express thoughts and feelings that I have myself. Let me give you an example."

He went to the den and came back with a

book, thumbing through it until he found what he was looking for.

"Listen to this," he said to Josh.

A heart that is distant creates a wilder-
    ness round it.
I pluck chrysanthemums under the
    eastern hedge,
Then gaze long at the distant summer
    hills.
The mountain air is fresh at the dusk of
    day:
The flying birds two by two return.
In these things there lies a deep
    meaning;
Yet when we would express it, words
    suddenly fail us.

He looked up at Josh. "That was written over a thousand years ago by a Chinese poet in a land about as different from ours as you can get, yet I know exactly what he's talking about. He could have written it yesterday. In many ways we've remained virtually unchanged for thousands of years. Sure, there are cultural and technological differences, but that's just icing on the cake. Underneath," he said as he put the book down, "we all still come from the same mold."

Josh finished making the sandwiches and sat down across from him. "I bet things were different in this room when you were a boy," he said, changing the subject.

"Not that much. We had a wood stove

rather than this gas one, and kerosene lamps instead of electric lights. Over there," he said, pointing to where the refrigerator now stood, "was an icebox. My father would bring blocks of ice home from the store during the summer to keep things cool. Then there was the bread." He sighed and thought back. "My mother baked fresh bread—it was a kind of ritual with her. When I was little, I used to enjoy sitting here and watching her. She would hum old Irish folk tunes to herself while she kneaded the dough. She could sing like a bird, but then I guess all children think their mothers have a beautiful voice."

"She was Irish?" Josh asked.

"Straight off the boat."

"Really? With an accent and everything?"

"Well, she tried to tone it down to fit in here, but that only made the subtleties of it stand out more. To me it's the most beautiful language on earth."

"Did she ever talk about what it was like growing up there?" Josh asked.

"Only once," he said. "I'll tell you about it if you like."

"Sure."

He waited while Josh opened his notebook and got out a pen.

"My father was five years older than my mother," Mr. Davis began. "She was only fifty-eight when he died of a heart attack. One spring day about a year later, I rode over here to see her and sat at this table while she made bread.

"My father's sudden death had aged her twenty years overnight, and she hadn't taken very good care of herself since he'd been gone. As long as I could remember she had always been vibrant and happy, but I hadn't seen a smile grace her lips since the day he died.

"After the bread was in the oven, she came and sat down across from me. Then she took my hands in hers, and bent her head as if in prayer. We sat like that for what seemed like a long time. I remember my mind wandering to the sound of a wood thrush outside in the trees. The lilting rise and fall of its two-part song sounded like a question asked, then answered, and unspoken questions filled the air between us. Finally, she raised her head and in a quiet voice began.

"She talked about what it was like growing up in Ireland: the poverty, the hunger, the feeling of hopelessness. Of people abandoning their country, not because they wanted to, but because there was no other way out. She also spoke of the good things: the sense of family and community, the ties with the past, and—hovering over everything else—the land. The transcendent beauty of the rolling green hills peeking through an early morning mist, the smell of the sea on a stiff breeze, and the light rain that drifted down as gently as snow.

"She came to this country full of mixed feelings: fear and hope, loneliness and longing. She talked about the long trip over with her older brother: the cramped quarters and cold sea air, the coughing of a woman sleeping near her, and the cry that went up when America was first sighted in the distance. They all rushed to the rail and stood there staring, not knowing if they were seeing the promised land or just another form of purgatory. She spoke of stepping off the boat in New York: the crowds rushing by her, more people than she had ever seen, everyone jostling and pushing.

"She went on and on, pouring out her soul into the sweet-smelling air of the kitchen. I felt like a priest listening to a confession. These were things she had never spoken of before to anyone and would never speak of again. This was her life. Not written on paper and printed for the whole world to read, but handed down in accordance with a much older tradition. Lessons learned and passed on from one generation to the next.

"As she spoke, I could feel the years of her life slipping away while the shadows outside began to lengthen. I felt like I was in a time machine, but not a mechanical contraption like H. G. Wells envisioned. No, this machine had been softened by the slow passage of the years, and colored with distance and love.

"Her brother was hired by Munson Steamship Lines and assigned to their Mobile office. They caught a company ship in New York and arrived here in the sweltering heat of summer. He would go to sea for months at a time while she waited in an unfamiliar city, very much alone.

"She spoke of the first time she saw my

father. It was at a dance for new arrivals in Mobile. He watched her for a long time from across the room while she stood in a corner, drinking punch with the other girls and pretending not to notice. The tentative way he finally asked her to dance with his eyes fixed on the floor. His appealing awkwardness as he stepped on her toes. The bouquet of wildflowers he picked for her on a church picnic, full of the sweet smell of jasmine and honeysuckle. The doll he won for her at the state fair by slipping the barker an extra quarter when he didn't think she was looking, then knocking over all the milk bottles with one throw. Their first kiss on a warm summer night, sitting on a bench overlooking the bay.

"They were married in a small ceremony attended by his family and friends. She wore a wedding dress that had been his mother's, its fine lace etched with tiny flowers. Her brother arrived unexpectedly at the last minute, just in time to give her away. The letter she had written him months before about her engagement had finally caught up with him in Havana, and he immediately transferred to another ship that was on its way home. They had a lazy honeymoon at an old hotel in Biloxi on the Mississippi Sound. She talked of having me, one of the most special times of her life. How she spent days just looking at me nestled in her arms.

"Then she paused, and I looked deep into her eyes. Through the wrinkled skin and graying hair I could still catch a glimpse of a girl running over the green hills of Ireland, a young woman staring off the bow of a ship, a wife saying her vows to the man she would stay with as long as he lived, and a mother holding a newborn baby to her breast. Layer upon layer of her life was peeled back and exposed one at a time, then fused together again into a unifying whole. One path taken through a potential maze of passages, one door opened from a limitless wall of choices, one drop falling into an infinite ocean. All of this was captured and imprisoned in the dark depths of her eyes.

"Everything built up to what she had brought me here to say. Something that had been bothering her, something that she felt she had to do. She wanted to return to Ireland, to see her family and the places of her youth one last time."

There was a long pause as Mr. Davis stared out the kitchen window, his eyes unfocused. Josh glanced up from the notebook and noticed that the old man's hands were trembling. The story he had been telling was still being replayed in his mind; it had just stopped bubbling up to the surface.

"Did she go?" Josh asked, breaking the silence.

"What?" He looked over at Josh with a start, as if he had forgotten the boy was there.

"Your mother. Did she go back to Ireland?" Josh repeated.

"Well, I tried to talk her out of it," he said, continuing. "Travel was dangerous by that time, with war looming on the horizon and German U-boats threatening shipping, but she was adamant. Finally, I gave in on the condition that I accompany her. She agreed. In fact, I think that's what she was hoping for all along.

"I talked to my wife about it, and she felt it was important that I should go. So I took a leave of absence from my job, and the two of us set out. We took the train to New York and from there booked passage on an ocean liner. It was an easy trip over, with calm weather and no sign of Germans, though it quickly became a hobby of most of the passengers to spend their days on deck watching for them.

"We landed in Dublin in a fog so thick you could barely see the dock from the ship, accompanied by the mournful sound of foghorns reverberating through the stillness of the harbor. I hailed a cab, found a hotel, and booked us two rooms. After we had unpacked, we went out in the city and ate dinner at a restaurant a few blocks away.

"The next morning we were up early and took the first train south. I listened absently to the people in our compartment as I sat by the window, unable to take my eyes off the passing countryside.

"Through the early morning mist, I could barely make out the shapes of houses and barns as they floated past. Then, about an hour out of Dublin, the fog began to lift, and the sun peeked out from behind the clouds. The train wound its way through a patchwork quilt of pastures and meadows bordered by low stone walls. When we would top a rise, I could see for miles in every direction, and no matter which way you looked everything was a brilliant green.

"And the light," he said, staring off into the distance and remembering it all at once again, "the light was different from anything I've ever seen. It diffused through the clouds, bathing the land in a soft glow. The fields seemed to radiate it back in almost garish shades of green that saturated houses, barns, roads, everything. Then suddenly there would be a break in the clouds, and the sun would slice through the air and illuminate the landscape like a message from the gods.

"Eventually, the rocking of the train and the warmth of the compartment caused me to doze off. I was awakened by the bump of cars and the sound of the train's whistle as we slowed coming into the station at Thurles. My mother hadn't wired ahead to say that we would be arriving, so there wasn't anyone there to meet us. In fact, she didn't tell me until then that it had been years since she had last heard from her few remaining relatives in Ireland.

"We got off the train and checked into a hotel. After unpacking our bags, we ate a late lunch at the hotel restaurant. Thurles is a small town, maybe five to ten thousand, and we spent the rest of the afternoon walking the streets and exploring the shops. It was the closest town of any size to her family farm, and as a girl she used to come in as often as she could. She remembered many of the streets and inquired at some of the shops as to the former tenants. Much had changed in the years since she had last been here, but much still remained the same, and she delighted in seeing all the old familiar places again.

"I'd noticed a change gradually coming over her since we'd landed in Dublin. Her previous fatigue and depression seemed to be lifting, letting the person I'd always known shine through again. Now, as we walked the streets of her youth, she was radiant, and I noticed that her accent seemed thicker. There was a gleam in her eye, and she smiled and laughed with the shop owners and people she met. Her pace quickened, and I had to work to keep up with her.

"We looked for a horse-drawn carriage and driver to meet us at the hotel in the morning and take us out to the farm where she grew up. It would have been easier to hire a car, but she would have nothing of it. In her day the only means of travel was by horse or on foot, and she didn't want a noisy piece of machinery spoiling the drive. I asked around and got the address of an old man who had a carriage for hire. We found his house, and he agreed to meet us at the hotel in the morning for the trip out.

"I knocked on my mother's door early the next morning and found her already up and dressed. She had been sitting by her second-story window, watching the day unfold in the town below since first light. We ate breakfast at the hotel and were waiting outside when Mr. Fennessey and his carriage arrived. He negotiated the narrow city streets with ease, weaving around parked cars and trucks and calling to people he knew as we passed. We rattled over a stone bridge that spanned a small river, and left the town behind us. The country lane wound its way through open fields and hills where cattle grazed peacefully.

"I had to admit that my mother was right, it is the only way to see Ireland," Mr. Davis said, looking at Josh. "Occasionally a car or truck would pass, causing a momentary racket, but then it would settle back down to just the sounds of the horse's hooves on the road and Mr. Fennessey's voice as he held forth on every topic imaginable. He loved to hear himself talk and needed little in the way of encouragement from our side of the conversation.

"The thing that fascinated me the most was the ruins. Hardly a mile went by that we didn't see an abandoned church or house from some bygone era to remind you of the long human history in that land. Often nothing remained but moss-covered stone walls that seemed to blend into the green fields around them.

"Several miles out from town, our driver reined in his horse and stopped by the side of the road. He pointed up the tall hill to our right. 'The oldest ruins in the county are on top of that hill,' he said. By craning my neck I could barely see a stone structure on the top. 'Put there when the world was still young,' he continued. 'No one knows who made it or why, but one thing is certain, it was here long before we arrived on these shores, and it'll be here long after we're gone.'

"We rode for several more miles through the sparsely populated land, occasionally passing someone on the road or in a nearby field. Then, as we rounded a sharp bend in the road, my mother stiffened. She tapped Mr. Fennessey on the back and told him to turn up the lane that led off to the left. He guided the carriage up the narrow track and continued on, the road climbing slowly upward. When it leveled off, he pulled his horse up short.

"My mother stood up in the open carriage, taking in the scene below. 'There,' she said. I followed her gaze along the lane that meandered down between the hills to a cottage in the distance. It was an idyllic scene straight off a postcard, with a thatched roof and white-washed walls. We continued down the lane and stopped beside the house. An oak tree shaded the swept dirt yard that was now overgrown with weeds. On closer inspection, I saw that the roof had rotted through in spots and the door hung open on its hinges.

"I helped her down, and she walked through the half-open door as two doves flew out a broken window, the whistle of their wings echoing off the vacant walls. I followed her inside and watched as she slowly moved through the deserted rooms. She stopped by the stone fireplace in the main room and knelt beside it, running her fingers through the cold ashes still in the hearth. As she got up, she wiped a cobweb from her face, leaving a smudge of ash on her forehead. She said nothing, but I knew that she was seeing everything the way it was, populating the empty house with memories from her past.

"After a few minutes, we emerged again into the yard. 'You didn't say you were a Murphy,' our driver remarked from the trough in the yard where he stood watering his horse. 'I could have told you that they moved away a few years ago.' He looked around him sadly. 'It's hard to make it on a farm nowadays, and the young ones don't have a love for the land like they used to.' My mother looked over at him without speaking. 'I'm not sure where they went,' he continued, tapping his forehead to try to jog his memory. 'It seems like it was Dublin or maybe it was London.'

"We walked through the yard, and she stopped at a rope swing under the lone oak. She sat in it gently, not sure it would still hold her up after all these years, and rocked back and forth.

" 'I came here with the thought of staying,' she said, looking up at me. 'But now I realize that home is more than just a place on a map, it's the people in it. People you know and love and who love you.' She took my hand, squeezed it, and smiled. 'I'm ready to go now,' she said. I helped her up into the carriage, and Mr. Fennessey turned back toward town.

"As we passed the hill with the stone ruin on the top, I asked him to stop so I could take a look. I left Mr. Fennessey discussing the fate of Western Europe, a topic—like every other—on which he had some very definite opinions.

"The day had turned overcast, with a hint of rain in the air. I hopped the wall by the side of the road and started up the hill through the thick grass. It was higher than it appeared from below, and I was out of breath by the time I finally reached the top. I was amazed to see that the structure, which didn't look that impressive from the road, was in reality taller than I was. It consisted of three irregular stones set in the ground to form the legs, with a huge flat rock laid across them for the top. The surface had been worn smooth by years of wind and rain, and it was pockmarked with eroded holes and crevices. It had stood on that spot for so long that the legs and top seemed to have fused together into one.

"The hill dropped off on all sides around me, and I felt like I was standing on a high mountaintop. I looked down at the carriage below, then out over the surrounding countryside, and I understood why the stones had been placed here. It was the highest point for miles, and the view was spectacular. Looking back, I could see Thurles in the distance, with the silver streak of the river running beside it. Farmhouses dotted the land, crisscrossed by stone walls. The wind at this height was blowing in from the ocean, and as I pulled my coat around me to ward off the chill, I had the uncanny sensation that I could feel the earth's rotation under my feet. It was as if the wind were standing still, and the hill on which I stood was rushing forward at a tremendous speed.

"While I stood there taking in the view, I became aware of a barely perceptible sound. It was a deep bass note that would swell, then fade. I couldn't quite place it, but now that my ears had become sensitive to it, it was all that I could hear. It seemed to come from everywhere at once; even the air and ground were humming. I looked for the source, and by chance put my hand on a leg of the ancient stone dolmen next to me. Immediately I jerked it back, as if I had received an electric shock, and looked at my hand in amazement. Then I slowly placed it back on the rock. The stone vibrated softly under my touch, and I realized that the sound was coming from the monument itself. It rose and fell as the wind gusted around it, like a child blowing across the top of a Coke bottle.

"The sound it made was old, as old as time. Its vibration resonated deep inside me, until I felt like a tuning fork that had been struck and left to ring. I closed my eyes, and the feeling of hurtling through space intensified. I felt like my anchor to reality had been pulled loose. Thoughts seemed to run through my head at the speed of light, building louder and louder to a crescendo.

"Finally, I opened my eyes and looked up at the prehistoric stones towering above me.

By the hands on my watch I had stood there for only a few minutes, but during that brief time I felt as if I had aged centuries."

Mr. Davis paused and stared at Josh. The boy felt his eyes on him and looked up from writing.

"There's something about being in the presence of mountains or great expanses of water," the old man continued. "Something in their vastness and beauty that channels the world into sharper focus. It wasn't merely by chance that Moses climbed a mountain to seek God or that a stone monument was raised on the desolate peak on which I stood. It wasn't an accident that Jesus stilled the waters or that this bay fills me with contentment. These places are sacred in a way no church can ever be. They're the last abode of a greater power—a power that makes us feel small and washes away our trivial worries.

"After a while I took my hand off the cold stone monument, which had been built in that forgotten place so long ago. I turned away from the sight of the distant hills and started back down the way I had come. The slope was slippery and steep, and, as with many things in life, coming back down was harder than the climb to the top.

"I reached the road and stepped back into the carriage. Mr. Fennessey turned and asked, half-joking, if I had seen any spirits up there. When I didn't answer, he gave me a questioning look. He must have seen something in my face, because he was quiet for a change. He just pulled his hat down low over his forehead, clicked the reins, and started down the road in the gathering dusk.

"I didn't look back as the hill faded into the distance behind me. I wanted to remember the vision from the top, not the bottom. Instead I looked ahead, to the next mountain I would climb or ocean I would cross. To the day when I would once again bear witness to the vastness and beauty of the world."

Chapter 12

One Small Pebble

We better get moving if we're going to make the game," Mr. Davis said, pushing his chair back from the kitchen table.

"Game? What game?" Josh asked.

"Didn't I tell you?"

"No," Josh replied. "You just said that you needed help with something this morning."

"Well, that's it."

"That's what?" he asked, still puzzled.

"What you're here to help me with. We're going to a baseball game," Mr. Davis told him as he began loading the picnic basket. "If we leave now, we can still make it in plenty of time."

Josh closed the notebook and came over to help him.

"Do you follow baseball, Josh?" he asked.

"Not really. I've watched a game or two on TV, but that's about it."

"Well, you're in for a treat, my boy. Now, if you'll put the ice and drinks in the cooler, we'll be off."

While Josh filled it, Mr. Davis hunted up baseball caps and lawn chairs. They loaded everything in the trunk of the Buick, and he handed Josh the keys.

"Why don't you drive, son. My reflexes aren't what they used to be."

Josh started the big car and drove slowly down the drive.

"And I thought *I* was a slow driver," the old man said with a chuckle.

"Which way?" Josh asked when he stopped at the end of the lane.

"To the city," Mr. Davis answered without elaboration.

"Where are we going?" Josh questioned as they drove down the winding county road.

"Spring Hill College, my old alma mater. I used to watch them play all the time when I lived in Mobile, but I haven't been to a game since I moved here. I thought it would be nice to go one more time."

They turned onto the interstate and were soon riding the seven-mile ribbon of elevated concrete over Mobile Bay.

"When I was a boy the only way across the bay was by boat," Mr. Davis said, turning to look out over the water. "Bay boats were a booming business, ferrying people and supplies to and from the Eastern Shore. Then the automobile came into its own, and the causeway was built."

He looked to his right at the low strip of land with a four-lane highway down the middle that paralleled the interstate.

"Yes sir, the causeway was a miracle of modern achievement in its day," he continued. "It opened up the Eastern Shore to anybody with four wheels and a seat. Sometimes traffic would be backed up for miles on a Friday afternoon. Of course, the bay boats all went out of business, and a lot of fine captains and crews had to find another line of work," he said, shaking his head sadly. "Then they put in this interstate, and it made the causeway obsolete overnight. Now by the time you can yawn, you're there."

"I guess that's progress for you," Josh said, changing to the left lane to pass a truck.

"I'm not so sure about that. You can kill a plant with too much water as well as too little."

"What does gardening have to do with it?" Josh asked, glancing over at him.

"Everything. People seem to have gotten the idea that technological advancement is always a good thing, always a step forward, but that's not necessarily true. With every improvement we make, we leave something behind. It's important to figure out what that something is before it's too late to get it back."

"But what's wrong with getting someplace faster?" Josh shrugged, fiddling with the radio dial. "What's the point of spending hours traveling, when you could be there in minutes?"

"If a goal is difficult to reach, it takes a determined effort," the old man answered.

"So?" Josh said, realizing that the radio was broken.

"Some of the most beautiful places have stayed that way simply because they were hard to get to. Take away that effort and everybody and their brother shows up, and before you know it they aren't so beautiful anymore."

"Like the beach?"

"Like the beach," Mr. Davis said, nodding. "I can remember when it was deserted, just miles of vacant sand and sea oats. You could walk all day and not see another footprint. Now, it's wall-to-wall condos and shopping centers. There are so many warm bodies packed together that a seagull can hardly find a decent place to land."

They drove on in silence, the open bay flanked on the right by the marshy delta. The water went by too fast to take in many details. Even the rich, musty smell of the salt marsh barely penetrated the closed windows of the car.

They cruised through the interstate tunnel that took them under the river and emerged again into sunlight on the other side. The interstate skirted around Mobile, avoiding the heart of the city, and they drove the eleven miles in as many minutes.

"Take the next exit," Mr. Davis said, pointing it out.

Josh turned off the busy highway onto Dauphin Street.

"Turn in here," he said after they had gone a little farther.

They passed through iron gates and up a winding drive flanked by a golf course.

"I never even knew any of this was here," Josh said, taking in the overhanging oaks and manicured lawn.

"It's a well-kept secret," Mr. Davis said with a smile. "You can park over there."

Josh turned into the parking lot and found an empty spot. They got out, unloaded the car, and walked across the lawn toward the baseball field. Even from this distance the old man's ears picked up the familiar sounds of the game.

There were no bleachers, only scattered groups of lawn chairs filled with the faithful. The field backed up to a tall stuccoed building from the 1800s. A net above the backstop fanned out to protect as many windows as possible from foul balls.

Mr. Davis directed them past the spectators and down the third-base line. A low chain-link fence provided some protection, but the threat of a wicked line drive was always present. They set up their chairs and watched the teams warm up.

"This is one of the oldest fields still in use in college baseball today," Mr. Davis said. "They call it 'the Pit' because of the way it's set below ground level on the first-base side."

He pointed to the old brick wall running along

the first-base line. A sidewalk paralleled it on the top, and students walked by, watching the proceedings with mild interest. Fans lined the wall, their feet dangling over the edge.

"Yes sir, this field is packed full of memories. Babe Ruth even played here once."

"Really?" Josh asked, looking at him with increased interest.

"He had a traveling team that went from city to city in the off-season to take on local ball clubs. When they came to Mobile he visited the campus, and Spring Hill's team talked him into playing a practice game with them. I was in school here at the time and was lucky enough to get to see him play."

"What was he like?" Josh asked.

"The Babe was everything you've ever heard about him and more. He horsed around with the players between innings; it was all just one big lark to him. I'll never forget the twinkle he had in his eye. A crowd began to gather as the news spread, and pretty soon people were standing all the way back to the parking lot. When he stepped out of the dugout for his first at bat, the fans went wild."

The old man's eyes roamed the field, remembering it the way it was.

"Ruth was used to being made a fuss over and stood there as big as a mountain until everyone quieted down. Then he turned to the crowd, tipped his hat, and said, 'I want to thank all of you for coming today, and I'll do my best to give you something to write home about. Now, if I can get your pitcher to put one right about here.' The crowd laughed as he held his massive bat out about waist high. Then he stepped up to the plate, settled into the batter's box, and was all business.

"Spring Hill had their ace pitcher on the mound, a left-hander by the name of Collins. His first pitch was a fastball that hummed in there pretty good for a called strike on the outside corner. Ruth never batted an eye. The infield yelled encouragement, and Collins turned to them and grinned.

"The next pitch was a wicked curve that hooked in toward the left-handed Ruth, then broke down and away for another called strike. The infield cheered as their teammate put the Babe behind in the count. Ruth stepped out of the batter's box and knocked the dirt off his shoes with his bat. Even though he was down in the count, he still looked totally relaxed, like he had been there a thousand times before. He turned to the coach, who was umpiring the game, held up three fingers, and said, 'You do get three of those in Alabama, don't you?' He replied, 'Yes, sir, Mr. Ruth, you sure do,' and the crowd hooted. 'And how many would that be now?' Ruth asked, scratching his head in mock seriousness, which brought on another outburst from the crowd. 'That would be strike two,' the coach said politely, holding up two fingers. 'That's what I thought,' Ruth replied, returning to the batter's box.

"Now, a more seasoned pitcher would have nibbled at the corners a couple of times, trying to get Ruth to chase one or get a good call from the ump. Collins, on the other hand, was like a peacock with his tail spread. He thought he had the big man right where he wanted him and decided to challenge him with a fastball right in the strike zone. Twice he shook his catcher off when he called for a curve, low and away. Finally, the catcher gave in and called the pitch he wanted.

"Collins reared back and put everything he had into it, and you could see the pitch written all over his face. The ball came in smoking, with a wicked hum. It started out looking like it would catch the outside corner but then tailed right back over the heart of the plate about belt high. Ruth went into that big easy swing of his, and I had the privilege of watching the ball disappear over my head from the best view in the house. Right out there," he said, pointing toward center field.

"Ruth turned toward the cheering crowd, his bat held up in one hand over his head. Then he planted a big kiss on it, handed it to the bat boy, and started a slow jog around the bases. As he rounded third, he looked over at Collins with a wink and said, 'Thanks, son. That's just about what I had in mind.'"

"You mean you played for the school when you were here?" Josh asked in amazement, eyeing the old man as if trying to picture the wizened body in a uniform.

"I sure did," he said, nodding toward the center fielder, who was dropping back, his eyes locked on a fly ball. "I owned that piece of real estate for three of the four years I was here."

"Things must have changed a lot since then," Josh said.

"Oh, not that much. One thing I like about this field is that they haven't added lights. All the games are still played during the day. Nature is a big part of baseball. The sun can be your friend if it's at your back or your enemy if it's in your eyes. It changes strategy, too. You know that if you can hold out just one more inning, the game will be called because of darkness. It makes it more alive, more real. When you put it under lights in an air-conditioned dome on artificial turf, you take away its spirit."

There was a metallic ping as the batter warming up launched one into left field.

"Now *that* is something that has changed," the old man said bitterly. "That infernal piece of pipe they call a bat today." Another pitch came in, and the old man winced visibly as the batter snapped a line drive between second and third.

"What do you mean?" Josh asked.

"I grew up with the music a well-seasoned piece of ash or hickory makes when it meets the ball. You could tell just by the sound whether the batter got all of it or just popped it up. To me a metal bat is like listening to cats fighting. I'll take the crack of a wooden one any day."

There was a squeal of feedback from the PA system, and the starting lineup was announced.

They stood as "The Star-Spangled Banner" was played, then the game got under way. Spring Hill was facing their crosstown rival, Mobile College. Both were small, church-supported schools, Spring Hill by the Catholic Church and Mobile College by the Baptists. It was fitting, really, that these two should be rivals. Historically the city had deep roots in Catholicism from the influence of the early French and Spanish colonists, and currently it was predominantly Baptist.

As the game progressed, Mr. Davis explained the finer points to Josh. After seven innings the score was tied at four apiece, and Mr. Davis opened the cooler and took out their lunch.

"Here you go," he said, handing Josh a plate piled high with food. "So, what do you think of the game so far?"

"I never knew there was so much to it—the strategy, I mean," Josh answered. "I always found baseball kind of slow and boring."

"A lot of people think that, but actually the pace is what makes the game so interesting." He looked at Josh, his eyes alive. "It's like chess, every lull has a purpose. If you're a player or coach, there's never a dull moment. You're constantly watching and thinking, trying to anticipate what will happen next. Even if you're just sitting on the bench waiting for your turn at bat, you have to be aware of what's going on. Watching the pitcher to see what pitch he throws in each situation, looking for what's working for him that day and what isn't, scanning the field to see how the defense is set up. It's really a thinking man's game."

Both teams sent only three men to the plate in the eighth.

"But much of it still seems to come down to luck, doesn't it?" Josh said. "I mean, you can hit it hard and only have an out to show for it."

"Right, and that underlying unpredictability is the other thing that makes the game so interesting to watch. There's a lot of skill involved in baseball, but there's a lot of luck, too. Even the best major league teams lose a third of their games. The best teams usually win, but sometimes fate conspires against them and unexpectedly they come up short."

Mobile College failed to score in the top of the ninth, leaving the game still tied.

"Come on, boys, you can do it!" Mr. Davis called as the lead-off batter for Spring Hill stepped to the plate.

"You don't really believe in fate, do you?" Josh asked.

"If you mean do I believe in divine intervention by the gods, the answer is no," he said with a smile. "But there are forces at work around us all the time that we will never fully understand."

Spring Hill drew a lead-off walk to start the bottom of the ninth.

"Like what?"

"Well, science has finally realized that unpredictability is built into everything that exists in the universe."

A sacrifice bunt moved the runner to second, for the first out.

"Now you've got 'em where you want 'em," Mr. Davis yelled, cupping his hands around his mouth.

"But I thought science works because it *can* predict what will happen," Josh countered.

"True, but science can only generalize, it can never really predict a specific case. On an individual level the world is a constant surprise, even to itself."

Mr. Davis turned his attention to the game. The next batter lined out to the second baseman, and the runner just managed to dive back to the bag to avoid a double play. Two outs.

"What does all this have to do with baseball?" Josh asked, still puzzled at the old man's logic.

At that moment, the batter hit a grounder toward the shortstop. With two outs the runner was going at the sound of the bat and had rounded third by the time the ball reached the infield dirt. It looked like a routine out at first and extra innings. But as the ball left the infield grass, it hit a small pebble kicked up by the advancing runner and took a bad hop— careening past the waiting glove of the shortstop to dribble into center field. The runner stepped on home, and the game was over. Josh and Mr. Davis stood and cheered as Spring Hill's team poured out of the dugout in jubilation.

"*That's* what it has to do with baseball," the old man said, turning to Josh. "The random placement of one small pebble completely altered the outcome of this game. It's the same way in life. Something as trivial as leaving here a minute earlier or later might decide whether we live to make it home tonight."

"What a gruesome thought," Josh said with a frown.

"It is unsettling, I admit. But usually small changes affect the course of our lives in much more subtle ways." They sat back down in their chairs as the players filed off the field. "When you're my age and look back over your life, you can see pattern and meaning everywhere. Not something as dramatic as predestination or a plan, but more like the pattern in the swirl of a cloud," he said, looking up at the sky. "You realize that everything that poured into your cup has blended together to form something unique, and that something is you."

They both sat quietly for a minute, staring out at the field. Finally the old man tore his eyes away and looked at the boy.

"What I'm trying to say, Josh, is that there are many paths you can take in life, and sometimes you'll get blindsided by something you didn't see coming. Take it for what it is, a pebble in the infield, and don't get bogged down thinking about what might have been."

He paused as he stared out over the new grass of the field.

"There will be other times," he continued,

"when you'll have to make choices on your own, and you won't always know which is the right road to take. When that happens, stop and listen to your heart. If you concentrate very hard, you'll hear a whisper deep inside that will light your way through the darkness and never lead you astray."

Chapter 13

Reflections

Josh and Mr. Davis folded their lawn chairs and walked back to the car. After loading everything in the trunk, Josh opened the driver's door to leave.

"Not so fast, son. I haven't showed you around yet," he said, motioning for Josh to follow him as he walked across the parking lot.

Josh closed the car door and caught up with him. As they walked along the sidewalk toward the center of campus, the old man talked about what it had been like when he was a student here.

"The twenties were a great time to be alive," he said. "We'd made it through the horrors of the First World War, and the Great Depression had yet to rear its ugly head. It was as if there were a break in the clouds that let the sun shine through for that one glorious decade.

We felt like we could do anything. The world seemed to be opening up like a flower, and we were there to pluck it."

Azalea bushes lined the walk, and the faded remnants of their blossoms littered the ground. Before them, the Gothic spires of the chapel rose sharply against the sky. Mr. Davis opened the door, and they walked inside.

The outside world vanished as the door closed behind them. The church was empty, but the smell of incense still hung in the air from an earlier service. They stopped behind the last pew.

"I spent many an hour here during my four years in school," Mr. Davis said. "There wasn't any of this 'come if you want to' approach they have nowadays. If you weren't on your deathbed, you were here when the church bell rang."

Josh's eyes followed the ornate moldings and vaulted ceiling, coming to rest on the figure of a crucified Jesus mounted on the wall behind the altar. It felt as if he had stepped back in time to another century.

"It's beautiful," he said as they slipped into a pew.

"Yes, it is," Mr. Davis replied. "Many of man's finer impulses have been channeled into religion, and some of his baser ones as well. I've no argument with the idea of paying tribute to the ultimate mystery. It's in the particulars that it breaks down for me."

Josh pulled out a hymnal from the rack in front of him, thumbing through the pages absently.

"You mean like different beliefs?" he said, looking over at him.

Mr. Davis nodded. "Mankind has been blessed with some true religious visionaries. They could feel the power that underlies the world and saw life as its wondrous manifestation. Each of them put his own touch on a similar message, like artists painting the same scene from different angles. I like to think that if they ever met, they would embrace each other."

The old man ran his hand along the worn pew.

"The problems arise with the followers," he continued. "They take his words, bending and twisting them until they're molded into a shape they can accept. Then they take the image of the world that he had so lovingly created and lock it away in a church where only the chosen are allowed to see it," Mr. Davis said bitterly.

They sat there for a few minutes, content in the silence around them.

"I've been thinking about what you said at the game," Josh said, bringing up something that had been bothering him. "How the world is basically unpredictable. But if that's true, then God doesn't know the future any more than we do."

"A good point," Mr. Davis replied.

"So everything that happens must be as much a surprise to God as it is to us," he said as he struggled to put his thoughts into words. "But if God doesn't know everything, then he's not really God."

"But if he does exist," Mr. Davis countered, "then maybe there's a good reason the world is designed the way it is. Perhaps God purposely sacrificed complete power and knowledge to free the world and everything in it."

"Free it from what?" Josh asked.

"From the oppressive weight of omnipotence," the old man answered. "To give the world and everything in it individual freedom. The freedom to think, to choose, to change, and to dream."

The old man stood up. "Come on, there are some other things I want you to see."

The sidewalk outside led past a mixture of old and modern structures.

"Many of these buildings weren't here when I was in school, and some of the ones I knew so well are gone. That's change for you. Even things as solid as these brick walls are fleeting when seen through the eyes of time."

"I like that," Josh commented. "Who said it?"

"Why, I did. Who did you think, William Shakespeare? No, it's not poetry, Josh, just a fact of life. But maybe that's all poetry really is, truth dressed up in fancy clothes."

He slowed his pace.

"No matter how much we wish it, things can never stay the same," he continued. "This college has weathered fires, hurricanes, and military occupation over the years. But each time it's gotten back up, rebuilt, and gone on about its mission. Why? Because teaching and learning are what life is all about."

They took a footpath down the grassy hill toward a small lake in the distance, the gravel crunching under their shoes as they walked.

"How old is this place?" Josh asked.

"The college was started by the Catholic Church in the 1830s. Members of the Jesuit order from France were recruited to run it. They only had about a hundred students in those days, now there are over a thousand. This whole part of the city is called Spring Hill, not just the college. It used to be considered out in the country until Mobile grew up around it."

They stopped in front of the lake.

"This is where it all started," he said, looking around him. "The spring that gave the school its name still fills this lake that the founding fathers built. They called it Mirror Lake because it was surrounded by trees and so still you could see your reflection."

Josh looked at the unkempt pond with weeds and algae growing in it.

"It doesn't look like much now," Mr. Davis said apologetically, "but in my day it was the local swimming hole and an important source of water for the school. Now it's neglected and exposed, but back then the only way here was by a path through the woods. It was a wonderful hidden place. There were wooden benches along the sides to sit on," he said, pointing, "and those rotting timbers you see in the middle are all that remains of the swimming platform."

"Why don't they keep it up and still use it?" Josh asked.

"Times have changed," the old man replied sadly. "This place has lost its purpose and meaning. City water and swimming pools have made it a forgotten relic of the past. It's too bad, though," he added. "This spring and the hill are the main reasons the school was built here in the first place."

Josh looked down at their reflections in the glassy water, then picked up a stone and skipped it across the surface. Their images disappeared as the ripples spread out in all directions.

They turned and started back up the path to the school, but halfway up the hill the old man stopped at a bench to rest and catch his breath.

"Mobile was built on swampy land," he said. "The heat and mosquitoes were unbearable during the hot months, so some families built summer homes up here to escape."

"Did it help?" Josh asked. "I mean, downtown is only a few miles away."

"I imagine it did," Mr. Davis said as he stretched his arthritic knees. "It's high enough here to pick up breezes that wouldn't be felt in town, and the humidity is lower away from the bay. But the big concern was the mosquitoes. Then it was more than just the discomfort of a few welts. With yellow fever and other diseases, a bite could spell sickness or death."

They continued up the hill, cutting diagonally across campus, and came to an antebellum raised cottage.

"It's beautiful," Josh said, looking at the afternoon sun gleaming off the fresh paint.

"I've always had a special fondness for this house," Mr. Davis told him. "It's called Stewartfield. Originally it was a separate residence, but now it's mainly used for receptions." He turned and looked down the long avenue of overhanging oaks that led up to it. "This is where graduation is held every spring. It's quite a sight to see the students walking down this lane in their caps and gowns."

They cut across an open green to an imposing brick building set well off the ground. It had a classical look to it, its gabled roof supported by an Ionic-columned portico. Mr. Davis climbed the steps and pushed open the door, ushering Josh inside. The main floor of the building was a large room with a vaulted ceiling. A row of tables lined each side of the central aisle, and tall Palladian windows captured the afternoon light. Students sat hunched over books or were busy writing.

"A library is a very special place," Mr. Davis whispered. "There's something in the air that feels different from anywhere else. I think it has to do with being close to so many books."

Josh looked around the sparsely furnished room. "But I don't see any books."

"Follow me," he said.

Mr. Davis walked down the aisle, and Josh followed him through a door into the stacks. Row after row of shelves were filled to the ceiling with books. They wound their way through the seemingly endless aisles until he stopped and closed his eyes, as if listening intently.

"Can you feel it?" he said, his voice sounding loud against the silent backdrop.

"Feel what?" Josh asked, looking around him, puzzled.

"Knowledge, son, the wisdom of the ages. We're at the heart of the collective memory of all mankind."

He reached out and pulled a book randomly off the shelf.

"Everything is here—philosophy, science, art, literature," he said. "And do you know what they really are?"

Josh shook his head.

"Every book you see around you is really a human mind, distilled down to its essence." He opened the book he held and thumbed through it. "Years of research and study, joy and pain, even life and death, are lovingly compressed into this final form. Books are written in blood, Josh, not ink," he continued. "Each one is a unique vision of the world with its own clear voice, like a song being sung a cappella. But put them all together under one roof and their voices intertwine, blending to form the sound of a heavenly choir. They're gifts to the world, just waiting to be opened and passed on to another generation. It's like Christmas any day you enter a library, and it's a little like being in church," he added, holding the book up in front of him.

"I never thought about it like that," Josh admitted, surprised at the old man's enthusiasm.

"It's true. And each of these writers have one thing in common no matter how different their thoughts. They all have the desire and ability to express in words what they learned in life, so the rest of us can share it."

He looked around him one more time. "We better be going," he said, returning the book carefully to its spot on the shelf. "I have something else I want to show you, and it's getting late."

They walked back in the direction they had come, past the chapel and across a side street. Mr. Davis guided Josh through a gate in a fence, then stopped. The land before them sloped down to row after row of ornate marble crosses.

"In my day most of the teachers here were Jesuits," he said. "Teaching was their calling, and many of them found a final resting place here." He gestured to the headstones in the cemetery before them.

They wandered down the rows until Mr. Davis stopped in front of one. The inscription read:

P. ERNEST J. BENDER, S.J.
NATUS 4 MAR. 1864
INGRESSUS 12 JUN. 1888
OBIIT 7 OCT. 1948
R. I. P.

"Father Bender is the teacher I remember the most," Mr. Davis said. "He taught English and literature. My father wanted me to major in business, so I did, but every chance I could I took a course under Father Bender. He was tough as nails, and I had to work hard just to keep up, but he loved his subject and it showed. I came to his funeral when he died, as did many of his former students."

"He must have been quite a teacher," Josh said, trying in vain to think of someone at school who had affected him that way.

"He was. Teaching was his passion, his life. I guess that's why I liked his classes so much. He loved a good argument. It didn't matter to him which side you were on as long as you felt strongly about it and could back up your opinions. I remember what he used to say when you went to him with a problem. Regardless of whether it had to do with class work or your personal life, Father Bender's answer was always the same."

"What?" Josh asked.

"He said that the key to finding answers to the questions that really matter in life isn't in how much you have or how much you know. The key that unlocks the door to understanding and happiness is in your perspective."

"You mean how you look at things?" Josh said, unable to believe the answer was that simple.

"Exactly," Mr. Davis replied. "It's like when you're out fishing in a boat. If you look over the side the sun is shining on, all you can see is a mirrored reflection of the world around you. But if you turn and look out of the other side of the boat, you can see deep into the water.

"What Father Bender tried to do was help us see through the surface to find what's hidden underneath. In the classroom he did it by urging us to look behind the author's words to see what he was really trying to say and how it applied to each of our lives. In life he had the gift of being able to lift his eyes higher and focus them further than anyone I have ever known."

The old man paused and rested his hand on top of the stone cross. "He also taught us not to confuse knowledge with wisdom," he said, looking over at Josh. "There's a difference, you know."

"I thought if you had one, you had the other," Josh said.

"No. Knowledge alone is hollow, just facts and figures that any computer can spit out. It needs wisdom to temper it, to give it meaning and substance. The world is full of knowledge—everybody with a Ph.D. has it. But wisdom is harder to come by. It requires a special insight and vision that few possess. Father Bender had that vision."

They walked slowly up the hill to the gate, then stopped and looked back. In the fading light, all the stones appeared the same. Josh raised his eyes and looked out over the city. From the top of the hill he could see for miles.

"Beautiful, isn't it," Mr. Davis said, standing next to him.

"I didn't realize we were this high," Josh replied.

"This view has come and gone over the years; at times the oaks have all but blocked out the sky. There was another hurricane when I was in school here, just ten years after the one I went through as a boy. As I walked around the campus after it was over, it looked like every tree here was bent and broken. Father Bender saw my long face and walked over to where I stood. 'Will,' he said, with that enigmatic smile that seemed never to leave his lips, 'you're still not looking deep enough.'"

"What did he mean?" Josh asked, mystified.

Mr. Davis paused, staring down at the ground. Josh was about to repeat the question when the old man finally looked up at him.

"I've been through three major hurricanes in my life, and their power is a frightening thing to behold," he said. "They take a lot from a place, not just in trees and houses, but in lives and dreams as well. But even they give something back in return."

He looked at the manicured lawns and flower beds that surrounded them.

"Hurricanes, like death, are nature's way of weeding out the weak and the old," he continued. "That may sound cruel, Josh, but in the process they make room for the new. When I walked around after the storm, all I could see was the destruction. I never took the time to look under my feet at the seedlings straining upward toward the light, and I never lifted my eyes high enough to see this view," he said, gazing off into the distance at the city far below.

Chapter 14

The Details

*T*he wind tugged at his clothes as Josh stood on top of the bluff overlooking the bay. His eyes traveled down the red clay of the eroded cliff to the water far below. As the first drops of rain fell from the dark sky, he closed his eyes and relaxed. He leaned precariously forward, feeling as though he could let go and soar on the wind. His center of gravity was balanced on the edge, when he felt a gentle nudge from behind—

"Josh."

He heard the sound of giggles and realized that the rest of the class was staring at him. Mark poked him again in the back, and he looked up to see Mrs. Strickland waiting patiently for an answer.

"Yes, ma'am?" he said, not sure what he had missed.

"I asked if you could tell us what Hawthorne meant when he said—"

The bell rang, and there was an instant scraping of chairs as everyone rose to leave. Josh breathed a sigh of relief and began to gather up his books.

"For tomorrow I would like you to read to the end of the next chapter," she said, raising her voice over the noise, "and be prepared to discuss it in class."

"Close call, genius," Mark said as he passed.

"And Josh," Mrs. Strickland said, "I would like to see you for a minute before you leave."

The classroom was empty by the time he loaded his pack and approached her desk. English was the last class of the day, and the hall outside was already thinning out. He stood with his eyes downcast, expecting a lecture, when he noticed the story he had written for last week's assignment on the desk in front of her.

"I wanted to talk to you about your story," she said, glancing up at him. "It's really quite good, Josh. I never knew you could write like that. Have you been holding out on me?"

He looked at her, relieved. "I don't think so."

"Well, it has real potential. There's a writing contest for high school seniors, and I would like you to submit it. The winner will be published in the newspaper, and—" She saw the look on his face and stopped. "What?"

Josh hesitated and looked down at her desk again. "I'm not sure I can," he said, his words trailing off.

"If you're planning on sending it somewhere else—"

"It's not that," he interrupted. "It's just that when I wrote it, I never really thought about it being published."

"What's there to think about?" she asked.

"It's sort of a personal story. I'm not sure I want other people reading it," he said as he fidgeted nervously with the strap on his pack.

"I see," she replied, unprepared for his

reaction. She looked down at the pages, a bit disappointed. "Well, think it over and let me know what you want to do." She handed the folder to him. "I've made some corrections on it, and it will have to be typed, double-spaced, if you decide to enter. Here are the rules."

He stuffed it in his pack and turned to leave.

"Oh, and Josh…"

"Yes, ma'am?" he said, stopping in the doorway.

"Try to keep your mind on school from now on. Okay?"

"Yes, ma'am," he said, closing the door behind him.

Crossing the parking lot, he saw Chris and Mark leaning against his car.

"She really let you have it, huh?" Mark said with a grin as he walked up.

"Not really."

"You mean you got off easy?" Chris asked.

"It wasn't that at all. You know the story we had to write?" Josh said, unlocking the car door and dropping his pack on the passenger seat. "She wants me to enter it in a contest."

Mark shook his head in disbelief. "And here we were taking bets on whether she hauled you into old man Howell's office."

Mr. Davis was sitting at the kitchen table, leafing through the *National Geographic* that had arrived in the afternoon mail, when Josh opened the back door.

"Anything interesting?" the boy asked as he put the old man's dinner on the counter.

"The same as usual," he replied, turning a page. "Distant lands and exotic animals. Which reminds me, how's our bluebird doing?"

"He finally started eating after a couple of days," Josh said, putting his notebook on the table and pulling up a chair across from him. "I actually think he's starting to get kind of fat now."

"What about his wing?"

"It's hard to tell with the splint on, but it doesn't seem to be bothering him."

Mr. Davis continued thumbing through the magazine. Josh sat there quietly for a minute, deciding how to bring up what was bothering him.

"I wrote a story for school that my teacher wants me to enter in a writing contest," he finally blurted out.

"Congratulations," Mr. Davis said, putting down the magazine and focusing his attention on the boy.

"But I'm not sure I want everyone reading it."

"Why?" the old man asked.

"Well, it's really about my family."

"And you're worried it'll hurt someone?" he asked.

"Yes, my mother."

Mr. Davis thought for a minute.

"Writing is about discovering what's inside of you, Josh," he said. "That's what really matters. I remember when I took a writing course at Spring Hill."

Josh opened his notebook.

"It was my first course under Father Bender...."

The chatter of voices died down as the priest entered the classroom. He leaned back on the front of his desk with his long black cassock hanging loosely around him. The room fell silent, but he waited a little longer before proceeding.

"I know you're all anxious to take this final exam so your summer vacation can officially begin, but I have a few things I want to say first."

He paused, organizing his thoughts.

"As most of you know, my field is literature. I only teach this writing course once a year, but of all the courses I teach, this is the one I look forward to the most." He looked around the room.

"Over the years I have found that there are two kinds of students who sign up for this course. Those who love to write and have been doing so for years, and those who just need another English course to meet their requirements for a degree and thought this one sounded easy."

The students glanced at one another, confirming the validity of his remark.

"As far as the first group is concerned, it usually contains one or two truly gifted writers. Sadly, the rest are merely dedicated and prolific, and in any creative endeavor these traits alone are never enough. Unfortunately, there is nothing I can say that will save them from years of disappointment at the hands of something they love.

"As for the second group, most of them dropped out after the first week or two. They quickly found out that creative writing demands something they are sadly lacking in, namely creativity. So I am really addressing these comments to the members of that group who are still with us today. Those few students who entered this class on a whim and found something inside them that they didn't know was there. They'll leave here today a little richer than when they entered."

His eyes scanned the room, sizing up each student.

"You've probably noticed that I haven't spent much time teaching technique in this course. If you don't possess the basic tools of writing by this point in your academic career, you never will. If you're an avid reader, then in all likelihood you've already unconsciously absorbed most of the technical abilities that you need. And if you're not, then becoming a writer isn't an option open to you.

"Instead, all I've tried to do is point you in the right direction. It's up to you to find the determination it takes to continue down that road. To take your thoughts and put them down on paper, breathing life into them."

He clasped his hands behind his back, pacing slowly back and forth down the aisles while he talked.

"And that is the essence of writing. When things go well, the words will seem to write themselves. Then, after you've cut and polished this rough stone for countless hours, you'll look down at it in amazement. Only then will you realize where the real power to create comes from, and I hope you will have the humility to give thanks.

"This course is not about grades, and what you do today won't affect them. You've all stuck it out and made an honest effort, and in a subjective course like this, that is all a teacher can ask. This examination is simply for your pleasure and mine, a last chance to express yourself in this class. It may take the form of an essay or short story in any style you choose. You will have two hours in which to complete it. The starting point—from which you may diverge as widely as you like—is this."

He turned and in a large flowing script wrote on the board, the chalk tapping loudly against the slate. After underlining it, he turned back to the class.

"'God is in the details,'" he said, echoing the words behind him. "You may begin."

Will stared at the board, turning over in his mind what Father Bender had said. When he was younger, reading had been an adventure to him. From the pages of books, he had come to believe that anything was possible. But as the years passed, the magic evaporated, and the books that had brought it were forgotten. His life became filled by the dull routine of school and a parade of part-time jobs. The bay, too, came to occupy a smaller and smaller place in his world, until it became a backdrop that he hardly even noticed.

College had come as a pleasant diversion, but the novelty had long since worn off. He was left with a nagging feeling in the back of his mind that something was missing from his life. Registering for the spring semester of his sophomore year, Will had stumbled on this class while filling out his schedule. He needed another English course, and creative writing happened to fit his available time slot. Father Bender had worked them hard the first few weeks, and, as he predicted, many of them had jumped ship. Will had almost pulled out with the rest, but there was something about the stern priest that held him fast.

At first he drifted along in the class, doing his work without any real passion. Then one night halfway through the semester all that changed. Their assignment was to write about their childhood. After supper he sat at his desk and thought back to the time he had spent growing up on the bay.

As he began to write, it all came back to him: the smells and sounds of the water, the wharf with his sailboat tied up next to it, lying on the porch in a hammock during a summer thunderstorm. The clock in his room ticked steadily through the night, breaking infinity down into finite parts, as his memories flowed out over the page.

Finally he put down the pen and flexed his ink-stained fingers. Rubbing his neck, he looked out the window of his dorm room at the break of a new day. Then he put his hand on the stack of pages in front of him and could feel their power. As he walked across campus on his way to class that morning with his paper tucked under his arm, the sky seemed brighter and bluer than he could ever remember.

Now, as he sat in class staring at the blackboard in front of him, he thought about the words Father Bender had written: "God is in the details." He had always thought of God as something remote and vague, more an idea than anything concrete. Something locked safely away in church and allowed out only on Sundays. And the details? Like the opening of a single flower or warm sand sliding between your toes? Like the feel of salt water when it dries on your back and the way the breeze ripples through the trees on a spring day? The little things that can slip by without notice or occupy a lifetime. The details. Add them all together and they become the world, but break them down and each is a world unto itself.

He took out his pen and started to write. The clock continued to tick on the wall above him, but he didn't hear it now. He was already somewhere far away, and the ticking had turned into waves lapping against a distant shore under a clear blue sky.

"That's the important part of writing, Josh, expressing yourself. Even if you're the only one who ever reads it," Mr. Davis told him.

154

Josh sat there staring at the notebook as he thought about what the old man had said. "I guess I better be going," he said, pushing his chair back from the table.

He closed the door behind him, and Mr. Davis returned to his magazine.

The door opened again a minute later, and Josh handed him a folder. "I thought you might want to read this," he said.

"I would be honored."

The old man waited until he had driven away before opening it. Then, as he settled back in his chair, his eyes followed the words across the page:

The door clicked shut and the boy stood in his room without moving, alone in the dark. Behind him, he could still hear the voices as they rose and fell, cutting through an angry sea of words....

Chapter 15

Rough Waters

The nagging drone leaked around the closed door to Josh's room early on Saturday morning. He was only half-awake, and it took a minute before he realized that it was his mother talking on the phone in the hall.

"Don't tell me again that it got lost in the mail. It just doesn't happen....

"I know, but—

"That's not the point, the point is that I—

"You know, *I* have bills to pay, too. It's not like we're—"

Josh rolled over, pulling the pillow on top of his head to try to block it out. He thought about the trip to Spring Hill with Mr. Davis: the baseball game, the library, the cemetery... But the words still managed to filter through.

"And what about him? You know he wants to—"

He remembered the time last winter when he stood alone on the rocks at the end of the jetty, looking out to sea. The waves crashed against it, sending spray high in the air and soaking him to the bone even through his jacket.

"I know he is—" his mother said, breaking into his thoughts again.

"Well, maybe if you acted like it sometime—"

He closed his eyes so tightly that he saw stars.

The receiver was slammed down hard, and he heard her footsteps retreating down the hall. He lay there for a minute, looking up at the ceiling, then rolled out of bed. After he had showered and dressed, he followed her down the hall.

She was sitting at the breakfast table, drinking coffee. He sat across from her, but she didn't look up.

"Let me guess," he said, starting to make light of the situation.

She glanced up, her red eyes and tightly pressed lips cutting him off. "I'll fix your breakfast," she said. She got up from the table and went into the adjoining kitchen.

Josh heard the rattle of pots and pans as he stared at the table.

"He asked about graduation," she said from the kitchen.

"Is he coming?" Josh asked.

"I should hope so," she said. "You *are* his son."

"What did he say?"

"He just asked when it was," she said, setting a glass of orange juice in front of him.

"I'm going to the beach today with Mark and Chris," Josh told her, and took a sip.

"Fine. I'll be filling in at the store anyway."

"It's too rough," Josh said. "There's not even a lull between sets."

"And look at the chop. You couldn't get a decent ride anyway," Chris added, nodding in agreement.

"You babies," Mark said. "I can't believe you're chickening out on me."

"There's a difference between being scared and being smart," Josh replied.

They were sitting on the deserted beach, watching the waves crash against the concrete pilings of the state park fishing pier.

Even though this was usually a popular spot with surfers, no one was out today.

"Well, I didn't drive all the way here just to sit on the beach," Mark said, hopping up and walking across the sand to the parking lot.

He unfastened the board from the roof of his car and walked down to the water's edge. On his knees in the wet sand, he waxed it, then attached the ankle strap and waded out into the water.

"Mark, wait," Josh said, catching up with him.

He continued to trudge through the water without stopping.

"Come on, Mark," Josh said, grabbing him by the shoulder to bring him up short. "You don't have to prove anything."

"Well, maybe you do," Mark said, shrugging off his arm and continuing out into the choppy water.

Josh stood there until Mark reached the first bar, then he walked back to where Chris was still sitting.

"We better go out on the pier and keep an eye on him," he said, extending a hand to Chris to pull him up.

They walked past the sign prohibiting surfing near the pier; since the waves were always better closer to the pier, the warnings were frequently ignored. This was a sore spot with fishermen, who thought that the surfers scared away their fish.

Josh and Chris walked up the slanted concrete walkway to the pier and stopped in the observation area. Only a few fishermen were scattered along the long pier. A bored concessionaire dozed on a stool behind the counter, and they bought ice-cream bars from him and leaned against the railing, watching Mark's slow progress through the surf.

Josh made a face when he bit into his and looked over his shoulder at the man behind the counter suspiciously.

"I wonder if they keep the bait and the ice cream in the same freezer?" he said, sniffing his wrapper.

"You and food." Chris sighed, shaking his head, "Why can't you just enjoy it like everyone else?"

Josh ignored the remark and nodded toward the small figure far out in the water. "He made it to the second bar," he said.

Mark was trying to pick his way through the surf, pushing his board under as each wave broke, then paddling furiously after it had passed. It looked as though he were losing ground every time.

"He just won't give up," Josh said.

Finally there was a lull, and Mark paddled quickly through.

"Well, at least he made it out in one piece," Chris said, licking a drip of ice cream off the side of his wrapper before it could run down onto his hand.

The current had pulled Mark closer to the pier, and they could see him clearly now. He bobbed up and down like a cork on the swells as he sat on his board, resting. Looking up at them, he held his hands over his head with his fists clenched.

"He'll never let us live this down," Josh said, waving back at him.

Mark turned and watched the swells building behind him. He decided on one and pushed off, dropping down the steep slope toward the bottom.

"He's not going to make it," Chris said as they watched him pick up speed, his board slapping against the choppy water.

Mark fought to retain his balance, his knees acting like shock absorbers. He reached the trough and turned, slowing his speed as he climbed back up the face of the wave, then pulling out just before it broke. Paddling quickly, he made it over the top of the next swell before he could be caught inside.

"Man, did you see that!" Chris said. "I thought he was a goner for sure."

"He's too close to the pier, though," Josh said, leaning out over the railing and looking at the concrete pilings with concern.

Mark realized his predicament and paddled away from the pier, gradually increasing the distance. Josh began to relax, and his eyes followed the pilings up to the top of the pier, where two men were fishing even with the surfer.

The one closest to him was carrying on an animated conversation with his companion. Josh was too far away to hear what was being said, but his sneering gesture in Mark's direction made his meaning all too clear. Josh watched as he changed the tackle on his big surf casting rod, clipping a snag hook on the end of the line. He nudged Chris without looking away from the fishermen.

"Keep your eyes on them," he said, nodding in their direction.

"Why?" Chris asked.

"I've got a bad feeling," Josh said, turning to look back out in the water.

Mark was paddling into position for another wave when the man on the pier reared back and cast as far as he could. Josh saw the hook plop in the water just past Mark, but Mark was too intent on the wave to notice. The fisherman reeled in quickly, then jerked back hard on the rod. Josh felt his stomach churn as he saw Mark pulled helplessly off his board into the water. The fisherman hooted with delight and leaned back against the rod, reeling steadily. As the waves washed over Mark, he floundered on the surface, driving the hook in deeper. He tried desperately to free himself before he could be dragged into the pilings.

"Jesus!" Chris said, his ice cream slipping from his fingers and falling over the side.

"Go call for help," Josh said to him as he pushed off the railing and started toward the pier.

Chris stood with his mouth open, not moving.

"Now!" Josh yelled over his shoulder. He ran through the open gate and out onto the pier.

"Hey!" the attendant yelled after him. "You have to buy a pass!"

The fishermen were so intent on their catch that they didn't see Josh until it was too late. Running hard, he lowered his shoulder and plowed into them, sending all of them sprawling.

Josh was the first one up. "Cut him loose!" he yelled to the man on the ground, who was still clutching the rod.

The fishermen struggled to their feet and turned to face him.

"You've got a lot of nerve, boy," said the man with the rod, scowling.

Josh saw the sinewy arms that protruded from his dirty T-shirt and realized he was out-matched.

"We was just about to land us a big one, when you come along not watching where you're going," the man continued, handing the rod to his partner.

He leaned down and picked up his faded baseball cap and put it back on without taking his eyes off the boy.

"It looks to me like you could use a little lesson in manners," he said, his eyes narrowing.

Josh backed up slowly as he approached, keeping his eyes fixed on his opponent. The man flicked a glance at the railing, and out of the corner of his eye, Josh saw a knife sticking up in the soft wood.

"I think you're a little out of your league here, boy," the man said, edging toward the knife.

"Hey!" the park attendant called, walking toward them. "You have to pay to come out here."

The fisherman made a move for the knife, but Josh beat him to it. Turning to face him, Josh held the knife out in front of him, and the man backed off.

"I said cut him loose," Josh repeated, waving the knife at him.

"Why don't you do it yourself," he said. "You're the one with the knife."

Josh hesitated and looked to the attendant for support, only to see him beating a hasty retreat to his office. Staying near the railing, Josh edged toward the line that ran over the side. The seconds ticked away as he debated what to do.

"What's it gonna be, boy?" the man taunted, keeping his distance.

Josh glanced over the side, tracing the path of the fishing line straight down into the water. Mark's board bumped against a piling nearby, but he couldn't see his friend. He looked back in time to see the man closing in on him, and he thrust the knife forward, keeping the man at bay. Realizing that he couldn't wait any longer, Josh whipped the knife across the taut line. It separated with a loud pop, and the fisherman holding the rod staggered backward. In one continuous motion Josh let the knife sail far out in the water and faced them unarmed.

"Now *that* was a bad idea," the fisherman said. "I think this is a good time for that lesson I promised you." His lips parted in a crooked grin as he started toward Josh.

Before he could follow up on his threat, Josh

vaulted the railing and plunged feet first through the air. The fall seemed to take forever, then he hit the water hard.

"Damn," the man on the pier said, looking over the railing at the trail of bubbles in the water far below.

"I think we've had enough fun for one day," his partner told him, gathering up their fishing gear.

The two men walked nonchalantly down the pier and through the turnstile

"Hold on, I want a word with you," the attendant said in his most authoritative voice as they passed his window.

The man with the cap gave him a withering look, and the attendant blanched visibly. They continued on to the parking lot, got in their pickup, and sped away.

Josh's feet hit bottom and he pushed off, breaking the surface only a few yards from Mark's board. A swell pushed him forward, and fire shot up his leg as he brushed against a barnacle-encrusted piling. He swam to the board, and his hand searched for the ankle strap that tethered Mark to it. Wrapping his hand around it, he pulled, and Mark floated to the surface a few feet away.

The hook was still stuck fast in his leg, and there was an ugly gash on his forehead. Josh struggled to work the limp body up on the surfboard and realized that his friend wasn't breathing. Wrapping himself around Mark, he used the surfboard for leverage and squeezed against him as hard as he could. Seawater poured from Mark's mouth, and he drew a ragged breath. Coughing, he opened his eyes.

Josh slid off the board and treaded water beside him.

"Listen, Mark, you've got to help me!" he said. "I can't get you in alone."

Mark raised his head and nodded weakly.

"You just hold on tight to the board, and I'll tell you when to paddle," Josh said as a swell tried to slam them into a piling.

Kicking from behind, Josh propelled them away from the pier, then turned the board toward shore.

"Okay. Now, paddle!" he yelled.

Mark paddled feebly while Josh continued to push them from behind.

They had almost managed to make it past the breakers when a wave crashed on top of them. Josh lost his grip on the board as the white water drove him to the bottom and held him there. He came up sputtering and frantically looked around for Mark. He saw the board's fin sticking up and was swimming to it when another wave took him under. When he came up the second time, he saw Mark break the surface beside the board and grab hold. Josh swam over to him and turned the board over, helping Mark back on it, then started kicking them to the beach again.

A small wave caught them as they neared the shore, helping them along, and Josh felt the board nudge against the sand. Exhausted, he looked up to see Chris running toward them. As his eyes closed, he heard the distant wail of a siren.

Chapter 16

───────── ❧ ─────────

The Waiting Room

*H*e was riding a wave that went on and on, seeming never to end. He heard the rumble of cascading water behind him and had to keep constant pressure on his board just to stay ahead of it. Crouched down, he could barely fit inside the walls of water. There was no room for maneuvering; it was one endless tube ride.

Soon he began to tire, and his back ached. He wanted to pull out but could never get far enough ahead of the curl. The mouth of the wave seemed farther and farther away, until all he could see was a small circle of blue sky closing like the lens of a camera in front of him. The roar of the water was gradually transformed into the sound of his own name calling him over and over—

"Josh," the nurse repeated, shaking his shoulder.

He jerked awake, breathing hard, as his eyes tried to focus.

"Are you all right?" she asked.

He saw the look of concern on her face and tried to answer, but nothing came out. He noticed the blanket draped over his shoulders and looked blankly at the white walls of the emergency waiting room. Then, in a rush, it all came back to him.

"Where's Mark?" he croaked, a note of panic creeping into his voice.

"He's fine," she said, patting his arm. "You can see him later if you like, but right now the doctor wants to take a look at you."

She helped him up, and his head began to clear.

"I'm okay," he said, but she kept a hand on his arm as she led him down the hall and into an examining room.

"Feeling better?" she asked after she had situated him on the examining table.

He nodded.

"The doctor will be with you in just a minute," she said, then closed the door behind her and left him alone.

He pulled the blanket tighter around him. His clothes had dried, but he still shivered in the cold room. There was a knock on the door, and a man with wire-rimmed glasses and a white coat entered, followed by the nurse.

"You must be Josh," he said, glancing at the chart in his hand. "I understand you and your friend had quite an ordeal today." He flipped through the pages, then looked at him. "How are you feeling?"

"Okay, I guess," he replied while the doctor shined a light in his eyes.

The doctor removed the blanket and poked

and prodded him. "Does anything hurt?" he asked.

"I don't think so," Josh said, then winced as the doctor touched his shoulder.

"Why don't you take off your shirt, and let's have a look."

Josh pulled it slowly over his head, realizing for the first time how sore he was. He reached for the medal around his neck, but it wasn't there. He looked around him frantically.

"Have you seen my medal?" he asked the nurse as he shook out his shirt. "It's a Saint Christopher on a silver chain."

"I didn't notice it on you when you came in," she answered, helping him look.

"I must have lost it when I jumped off the pier," Josh said. His shoulders sagged, and he closed his eyes.

"I'm sorry," she said. "You can buy another one in the gift shop in the lobby," she suggested, trying to be helpful.

"It wouldn't be the same." He sighed. "My father gave it to me."

The doctor examined his shoulder carefully. "It looks like a bad bruise," he said. "But we better take an X-ray just to be sure. What happened here?" he asked, inspecting the raw spot on Josh's leg.

"I guess I rubbed it against a piling on the pier," he told him, noticing it for the first time.

The nurse reached into a cabinet and got out bandages and a bottle of antiseptic. Josh gritted his teeth as the doctor poured it over the wound and bandaged him up.

"Scrapes like this can get infected easily, so I'm going to give you something for it," he said, holding up a syringe.

Josh flinched as the needle went in his arm.

"Anything else bothering you?" the doctor asked as he disposed of the syringe.

Josh shook his head. "How's Mark?" he asked.

"Your friend was pretty banged up and needed a few stitches. We're going to keep him here overnight, but if he doesn't develop any respiratory complications, he should be able to go home tomorrow."

He handed Josh a vial of pills from the cabinet. "Take these for your leg, and come back to see me if it gives you any problems."

Josh returned to the waiting room and was about to sit down when he saw his mother coming in the door. She saw him at the same time and ran over, throwing her arms around him. Josh drew in his breath sharply as she hugged him.

"You're hurt!" she said, stepping back.

"I'm okay," he said, pretending it hurt less than it did. "The doctor thinks it's just bruised, but they're going to take an X-ray to be sure."

"Chris called me at work and told me what happened," she said. "I got here as soon as I could."

They sat down, and he told her the whole story. She refused to let go of his hand, squeezing it harder as he went along.

"That was a very brave thing to do," she said when he finished. "But you were lucky. You could have been seriously hurt, or worse."

"I know. But if I hadn't done it, Mark wouldn't have made it," he said.

"You don't know how I worry about you, Josh," she said, brushing his hair back out of his eyes. "I guess I always will."

"We're ready for you," the nurse said, waiting to take him for his X-ray.

He got up and started to follow her, then stopped and walked back over to where his mother was sitting. Leaning over, he kissed her cheek.

"I'll be right back," he said.

He saw the strain on her face and waited until she looked up at him. "Everything turned out okay," he told her. "That's what matters."

Then he followed the nurse down the hall.

"The X-rays came out negative, Josh, so you're free to go," the doctor said, stopping by the waiting room. "You're going to be sore, so just take it easy for a couple of days and you should be fine."

"Can I see Mark now?" he asked.

"Of course," the doctor replied. "Ask the receptionist in the lobby for his room number."

"Thank you for everything," Mrs. Bell added.

"I'm going to check on Mark," Josh said after the doctor had left. "I'll be home in a little while."

"Do you want me to wait and drive you home?" she asked.

"That's okay. Chris drove my car over here and left it in the parking lot."

"Well, don't stay long," she said.

Josh walked down the endless corridors of the hospital, looking for Mark's room. Some of the doors were open, and he caught glimpses of patients lying in bed as he passed. Their hollow eyes stared back at him or were fixed on the glow of the television set mounted above each bed. He finally found the room and knocked softly on the door. Mark's father opened it.

"Come in, Josh," Mr. Johnson said solemnly.

Mark's mother was sitting in a chair by the bed and got up to give him a hug. She started to say something but broke down before she could get the words out. Instead she motioned him over to the bed.

"Mark, Josh is here," she said, patting her son's hand gently.

Mark's eyes were closed, and the cut on his forehead had been bandaged. Slowly he opened his eyes and looked at Josh.

"Well, if it isn't my guardian angel," he said weakly, holding his hand out.

"How's it going?" Josh asked as he took it.

"Great," he said with a wan smile. "I feel like I've been run over by an eighteen-wheeler." Once again his eyes closed, and he drifted off.

"They've given him something to make him sleep," Mrs. Johnson whispered.

"I just wanted to see how he was doing before I went home," Josh said, turning to leave.

Mr. Johnson followed him out in the hall and closed the door behind them.

"We heard what you did today, Josh," he said. "I'll never be able to thank you enough."

"Mark would have done the same for me," Josh said, a little embarrassed. "That's what friends are for."

I guess Mr. Davis was right, Josh thought as he drove home. In an instant your life can be changed forever. He remembered the vacant eyes he had seen in the hospital rooms and wondered what stories they held. Then he thought about the chairs that lined the walls of the waiting room, constantly filled with pain and sorrow.

Instinctively he reached up to rub the medal his father had given him, then he remembered it was gone.

Chapter 17

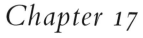

Silence

From his house the old man walked south along the shore in the morning light, his shoes leaving a trail of perfect impressions in the damp sand. He listened to the sound of the water lapping against the shoreline as he made his daily journey to the distant point of land that jutted out into the bay. To the north new houses had been built, their impeding seawalls trying to hold on to the fragile land the bay always seemed ready to reclaim, but here the land was too low to be built upon.

It was not just practical reasons that turned him south but spiritual ones as well. The centrifugal tug of the equator and the ebb of the tide reached deep inside him, urging him on. When he reached the point, he would sit on a log that had washed up years ago, alone with his thoughts. From this vantage point he could see much of the coastline of the Eastern Shore and watch the ships far out in the channel. Often he would sit peacefully for hours, thinking and remembering.

The point was still a quarter of a mile ahead this morning, his shoes squeaking against the sand with every step. He had read once that you could tell much about a man by the footprints he left behind. European settlers had walked with their feet splayed outward, dominating the world and bending it to their will. Indian footprints, however, pointed straight ahead or slightly inward as they threaded their way through life, respecting its balance and conforming to its rhythms. As a boy he had spent hours practicing walking in the Indian way, and whenever he caught himself unawares he would stop and check the trail behind him to note his progress. Even now he paused to glance back at his footprints in the sand and smiled. Old habits die hard, he thought.

His pace was slow but steady. Lost was the energy of youth, but in its place arose a tenacious desire to absorb everything around him. He took it all in, leaving nothing out: a beer can rolling back and forth at the water's edge, a dead catfish covered with flies and ripening in the sun, a piece of driftwood left high and dry by the tide the night before. The silence was complete, and the white noise of the bay only added to it.

He thought of Josh, and the story he had written. It was full of pain and loss, and he could tell it came straight from the boy's heart and life. He understood now why he was reluctant to let others read it.

A movement in the grass to his left caught his eye, and he stopped. The grass wavered slightly, leaving a trail as fleeting as the wind. The ripple neared a small clearing, and the old man stood motionless: watching...waiting. For what seemed like an eternity nothing happened. Then, in a blur of liquid motion so quick it barely registered on the human eye, a field mouse darted across and disappeared into the high grass on the other side.

Mr. Davis continued on toward the point along the deserted shore, and the image that he was the last man on the face of the earth came over him. He was almost there now, his eyes searching the sand for gifts the tide might have deposited. He looked up as a distant, barely audible hum intruded on his solitude. Shielding his eyes, he looked toward the point as the sound became clearer. The irregular buzzing, like the wings of a gigantic insect, grew louder by the second. He stopped and stood by the water's edge, waiting for it to materialize.

Two Jet Skis careened around the point at breakneck speed a hundred feet from shore, cutting across each other's wakes and spinning three-sixties in the shallow water. Their engines whined as they churned up the soft mud, turning the bay around them chocolate brown. A heron squawked and took off from the shallow water it had been fishing. Mr. Davis watched, anger seething inside him, as the still and quiet of the day evaporated. What a waste of time and money, he thought, but mostly what a waste of silence.

The old man turned, short of the point, and walked slowly home, his eyes downcast in defeat. The day, which had started out so promising, was ruined. Behind him he could still hear the clash of engines as they echoed off the water, and it seemed as if the air itself shuddered at their discordant sound.

Chapter 18

Checkmate

The car rolled to a stop next to Mr. Davis's Buick, and the driver uncoiled himself from the front seat. Balancing a box of doughnuts in one hand and two coffees in the other, he nudged the car door closed with his hip, then walked across the drive and up the steps. He looked at the door, then down at his hands, and called through the open screen.

"Hello...anybody home?"

Mr. Davis put down the book he had been reading and got up from his chair in the den. Peering through the screen, he tried to put a name to the shadow standing in the doorway.

"I come bearing food and drink," the shadow said in response to his questioning look. "That are still warm, I might add."

The old man's face lit up. "Well," he replied in his best imitation Irish brogue, "if it isn't Father Michael O'Ferrall, out making the rounds on his elderly lost sheep."

"I keep telling you, Will, that my family has been in this country since the 1800s. All I know of Ireland is what I've seen in *The Quiet Man*," he said, shaking his head. "So, are you going to let me in or leave me standing out here all day?"

"No, I fully intend to open the door just as soon as you promise me that you won't try to twist my arm again about coming back to church."

"You know I gave up on you years ago."

"Promise?"

"I've got Krispy Kreme doughnuts and coffee," the priest said, holding up the box where Mr. Davis could see it.

"Bribery will get you everywhere," Mr. Davis said, pushing open the screen door.

Father O'Ferrall set the box and coffee on the kitchen table. After removing the lids, he handed a cup to the old man.

"Here you go, cream and sugar, just the way you like it."

"Thank you," Mr. Davis said and took a sip.

He opened the box of doughnuts and held it out to his guest.

"I'm never going to lose weight if I keep having to bribe you," Father O'Ferrall said as he hooked a long index finger through the hole in the center.

They walked out onto the porch. Mr. Davis put the box on the table between them and eased into his rocker.

"Ah, just what I needed," the priest said, sitting down and looking around him. "I envy you, Will, having this splendid view seven days a week. No worries, no hassles, no parishioners."

"It's peaceful all right, but there's a down side, too."

"I can't imagine what," Father O'Ferrall said, reaching for another doughnut.

"Well, for one thing it gets lonely at times.

Why, just the other day I caught myself carrying on a spirited conversation with only the four walls as an audience," he said.

"We all talk to ourselves. It's what keeps us sane," Father O'Ferrall replied.

"But when you start doing it out loud, you begin to worry."

"I wouldn't give it another thought," the priest said with a smile. "When you're as old and senile as you are, talking to yourself must come naturally."

"Ha! I may be old, but I've still got enough left upstairs to go a few philosophical rounds with you without even breaking a sweat."

"Not today, Will," Father O'Ferrall said. "I'm feeling kind of fragile myself, and I don't need you asking me to explain again why a church that's devoted to the virtues of poverty has so much."

"I won't give you a hard time, Michael. Besides, it's too easy anyway. There's no sport in it."

"That's reassuring," the priest added sarcastically.

"You haven't been by lately," Mr. Davis said. "The church must be keeping you busy these days."

"It's always something with a small parish: confessions to hear, parishioners to appease, baptisms, weddings, funerals...the list goes on and on. Sometimes I can barely find time to think, much less pray. Lately, I've been trying to keep the beige and green factions in the Parish Hall carpet dispute from each other's throats," he said, and took a swallow of lukewarm coffee.

"You've chosen a hard line of work in which to find inner peace," Mr. Davis said. "It would have been easier if you'd become a fisherman, alone in your boat with only the sea and the sky for company. Fish are simple creatures: they eat, swim, mate, and die. Our lives revolve around the same agenda, we just work at making it as complicated as possible," he said with a smile. "It sounds to me like you're spending most of your time untangling a backlash from someone else's line."

He took another doughnut from the box on the table and chewed it thoughtfully.

"You know, the funny thing is that I became a priest for the spiritual side of it," Father O'Ferrall replied. "Oh sure, I like helping people, and it can be very rewarding at times. But I often feel like I'm drowning, being pulled under by the very people I'm supposed to help. Why, just last night I woke up in a cold sweat from a dream I had."

"What about?"

"Well," he said, thinking back. "I was in the pulpit at church, giving a sermon. In the middle of it a member of my congregation stood up and started walking toward the front of the church. Then, one by one, everyone else did the same thing. They formed a circle around me and just stood there, staring up at me. I went on with my sermon like nothing had happened, but they started pressing closer and closer until I could hardly breathe,"

Father O'Ferrall said with a shudder. "Then I woke up."

"Well, you don't need Freud to interpret that one for you. It sounds to me like you could use some time off."

"I've got a vacation coming up soon. Hopefully by then the carpet debate will have worked itself out."

"You know, Michael, most of my life has been filled with the same things you're dealing with now."

"How?" Father O'Ferrall snorted. "Unless I missed something, you were never a priest."

"No, but I've spent a lot of time dealing with people. It's not that different. I lived in a world full of appointments, meetings, and disgruntled customers just like you do. When I retired and moved back here, I actually thought I would miss it all. But after a few months, I couldn't imagine living anywhere else. Life here has a whole different feel. You're anchored to something you can get your arms around, not just a stack of papers. If there's one thing that living here has taught me, it's that life is far too short for it to fly by in a non-stop blur. You have to slow down and let things take their course, find the time to know who and what you are."

"But I'm supposed to be the rock these people depend upon."

"It's hard being a rock," Mr. Davis said with a deadpan expression.

"Nice pun, Will."

"The trouble is that people *aren't* rocks,

they're delicate creatures that bruise far too easily. You don't need to harden yourself, Michael. You need to learn to flow around them like water, gently washing away their troubles."

"That's not easy when everyone constantly wants something from you. I'm always supposed to be there for them, but who's there for me?"

"No, it's never easy, whether you're a businessman or a priest. Just remember that what your congregation wants and what they need are two different things. What they want is someone flawless to tell their troubles to, who also happens to be an efficient businessman and a social butterfly. But what they *need* is simply someone connected to powers greater than themselves. Someone who spends time contemplating the infinite while they go about the day-to-day business of making a living and raising a family. Someone who can draw them together and make their petty problems vanish in a moment of beauty and light. Your task, first and foremost, is to know God. Everything else springs from that."

Father O'Ferrall stared vacantly at the floor, then he looked up and nodded. "You're right."

"Of course I'm right—haven't you learned that yet?" Mr. Davis said, slapping him on the knee. "Now, how about a game?"

"Sure."

Mr. Davis went inside and came back carrying a wooden box and chessboard. He set the board on the table between them and placed the box next to it. They got out the worn ebony and maple pieces and arranged them on the board, then Mr. Davis hid a pawn in each hand and held them out in front of him. Father O'Ferrall tapped his left hand, and the old man opened it to reveal the black piece.

"Not again!" the priest complained. "You always go first."

"I guess it's the luck of the Irish."

"But I'm Irish, too," he countered.

"Yes, but I've actually been there," Mr. Davis said, moving his king's pawn forward two spaces.

Father O'Ferrall responded by bringing out one of his knights.

"I saw an old Volkswagen leaving here the other day when I drove by," the priest said casually.

"I've had a boy out here helping me in the afternoon," Mr. Davis replied, moving his bishop diagonally toward the center of the board.

"Oh?"

"Josh Bell. His mother has the 'meals on wheels' business. Josh delivers them for her after school."

"Bell? Isn't she the one who filled in at the library last year?"

"That's right." He moved his queen out diagonally in the other direction.

"Don't even *think* of trying that old trick, Will."

"I was just seeing if you're paying attention."

"Maybe it's you who isn't paying attention," Father O'Ferrall said, attacking with his knight and taking the pawn in front of the queen's bishop. "Check."

"Now *that* was uncalled for," Mr. Davis chided. He moved his king out of harm's way, leaving his rook open to attack.

"I remember her because she helped me find some information on the early French missionaries in this area. She seemed very nice." He took the old man's rook with his knight.

"Josh is a good kid, too. He's a senior this year," Mr. Davis said, moving his queen.

"What have you got him doing? Mowing the grass and trimming the bushes?" he asked, bringing out his other knight.

"No, writing."

"Writing?" Father O'Ferrall repeated, glancing up at him.

"You know, pen and paper, words on a page, that sort of thing."

"I know *how* it's done, I was wondering more what and why."

"Oh, just something I've been meaning to do."

"Well, if you don't want to tell me the real story, I can't make you."

"The real story is that he's a good kid who's a little lost and isn't sure which way to turn."

"And since when did you become a guidance counselor?"

"We all need a little push in the right direction every now and then—even you, Michael." He picked up his queen and paused with it in his hand. "You know the difference between you and me is that while you're content with a piece of the pie, I've got my eyes fixed on the whole dessert cart." He put down his queen with a flourish. "Checkmate," he said triumphantly.

The priest's mouth dropped open, and he studied the board intently for a way out. Finally he threw up his hands in disgust. "Well, you've done it again, and just when I thought I had you on the ropes."

"By the way, I've got something for you," Mr. Davis said. He got up and went inside, returning a minute later with an envelope, which he handed to the priest.

"What's this?" Father O'Ferrall asked, looking at his name written across the front of it.

"You might not have noticed, Michael, but I'm not getting any younger. When my time comes, I want you to be the one there to see it through. I know I can count on you to carry out my wishes."

The priest stared at the envelope in his hand, a slight frown playing across his lips as he pondered the possibilities. Then he looked up at the old man.

"I would be honored, Will," he said, his frown turning into an uncertain smile. "I'm sure it will be a unique experience. But don't plan on going anywhere soon. I demand a rematch first."

Chapter 19

Hidden Inside

As he made his deliveries on Monday, Josh couldn't stop thinking about what had happened over the weekend. On the drive between houses, images from the pier kept replaying themselves in his mind. He hadn't slept much the last two nights, and it was starting to catch up with him.

Mark had been released from the hospital on Sunday, and Josh and Chris had stopped by to see him later that afternoon. He already seemed like his old self and even gave them a hard time about missing the big waves at the pier. Mrs. Johnson brought them a pizza and hovered over Mark, asking him if there was anything else she could do. After she left, he told them that he was going to drag out his recovery as long as possible, but he would be back at school before graduation on Thursday.

Josh turned in the drive to Mr. Davis's and was halfway down it when the VW's engine cut out on him. It had been acting up lately, and rather than trying to restart it, he put the car in neutral and coasted the rest of the way to the house. After rolling to a stop, he leaned back in the seat and closed his eyes, listening to the sound of the water. He had almost drifted off when the fisherman's malicious grin appeared again, floating in the blackness.

Giving up, he opened the car door and climbed the steps to the house. He left the dinner on the kitchen table and walked out onto the front porch, looking for the old man. Shielding his eyes against the afternoon glare, he saw Mr. Davis sitting on the end of the wharf and went out to join him.

"I didn't hear you drive up," Mr. Davis said as Josh sat next to him. "Maybe my hearing *is* starting to go after all."

"Your hearing is fine," Josh replied. "My engine died, so I coasted the rest of the way."

"Nothing serious, I hope."

"I don't think so," he said. "The carburetor probably just needs adjusting again."

"So, how was your weekend? Did you go to the beach?"

"We went surfing on Saturday," Josh said, "but we caught a lot more than just waves."

Starting from the beginning, he told Mr. Davis the whole story.

"I just don't get it," Josh said when he had finished. "Why would anyone do something like that?"

The old man didn't respond right away. Instead he looked out over the bay. In the distance a sailboat leaned hard against the wind, its sails suggesting a rigidity they did not possess. From their vantage point the boat appeared to be barely moving, but the shower of spray it sent up told a different story.

"We live in a world of infinite possibilities, Josh, for both good and bad. Each of us is a hodgepodge of millions of years of collective evolution, kind of like that old car of yours. We've been patched and tinkered with so many times that it's a wonder we even run at all."

"But nobody *made* him do that to Mark," Josh said.

"No, but most of the choices we make in life aren't as random as the pebble in the baseball game. They're constantly influenced by who we are and where we've been."

"But you said before that we had the freedom to choose, and now you're telling me that we don't," Josh said, shrugging. "You can't have it both ways."

"Why can't you?" Mr. Davis replied. "Your car has to have gas and air to make it run, but without a spark to set it off, nothing would happen. Freedom is that spark, Josh. But everything else that goes into it is important, too, if you want it to run right."

Josh thought about it for a minute, then shook his head.

"I understand what you're saying," he said. "But it doesn't make what happened to Mark any easier to take."

"No, it doesn't. Often it seems like the questions we're faced with are koans that we'll never understand."

"Koans?" Josh asked.

"A paradoxical statement that has no simple answer. I guess the most well-known one is 'What is the sound of one hand clapping?' "

"But one hand *can't* clap," Josh said, puzzled.

"Exactly."

Mr. Davis leaned forward and lowered his voice. "I'm going to tell you a secret that took me a long time to figure out."

"What?" the boy asked, leaning forward himself without realizing it.

"Life is a mystery, Josh, and it always will be. Why we're here and what's at the end of our journey are riddles we were never meant to solve."

Josh sat back in his chair, unimpressed.

"So everything we do is just a waste of time?" he asked.

"No, quite the opposite. When you reach my age, you suddenly realize that what really matters is not getting there, but the sights you passed along the way. Everyone is so worried about the future that they don't take the time to enjoy the present. It's like in school when students care more about their grade than learning what the course has to offer."

"I guess I've been guilty of that, too," Josh said.

"Speaking of which, have you decided about college?" Mr. Davis asked.

"Well, I've been accepted, but I didn't get a scholarship," Josh said with a note of resignation in his voice. "So I guess I'll be looking for a job after graduation."

"You can always get financial aid and government loans."

"But I'll be so far in debt that I might never get out," he said.

"A good education is one of the most important things there is, Josh. It's worth whatever it takes to see it through."

"But what if I don't make it?" he said. "I mean, I'm not exactly an honor student."

"I read your story," Mr. Davis told him. "You've got a special gift. You're not going to be happy pumping gas or cooking fries. You owe it to yourself to find out what's hidden inside of you, waiting to come out. But you'll never know unless you try."

Chapter 20

Night Sounds

The earth creaked and groaned like a worn-out hinge as it wobbled around the sun on its axis. Finally the days began to settle down into a more regular rhythm, and spring's transition became a fading memory. The sun inched higher in the sky with each passing day, painting the elongated shadows of winter into a corner. It hung suspended above the horizon a little longer every evening, warming the days with a heat that dissipated rapidly as night descended.

Young children stayed out later, their games growing louder as they tried unsuccessfully to tune out their mothers' calls in the deepening twilight. Teenage girls shed their confining winter clothes and crowded the pools and beaches, basking in the warm sun. Their pale bodies slowly turned brown while they hid behind sunglasses and romance novels, outwardly ignoring the watchful eyes of boys.

The cool night air seeped through screens on open windows, and sounds traveled easily without the constant noise of air conditioners to drown them out. In the stillness, a dog barked nervously at the unseen snap of a twig, and frogs called to one another across backyard ponds.

It was well after midnight, but Josh couldn't sleep. He had been lying in bed for over an hour, staring at the ceiling. Tomorrow night was graduation, and he had to admit that he was a little apprehensive. It wasn't so much the ceremony that bothered him, but the fact that tomorrow divided his life in two as sharply as a razor.

That image made him think back to the time he was five and had been playing with his father's razor while taking a bath. He had been pretending to shave, as he had watched him do so many times before. But when he looked down, the water around him was tinged red. He put his hand to his neck, pulled it away, and saw the blood. He called out in panic, and his mother opened the door. A look of horror crossed her face as she saw him sitting there, the razor in one hand and blood in the other.

"Jesus! What have you done!" she said sharply, rushing over to the tub.

"I—I was just playing, Mom," he said without thinking.

He began to sob quietly. Not from the pain, because there wasn't any, but in response to his mother's reaction. Was he going to die? Bleeding to death while she looked on helplessly? She washed out the cut tenderly and held a towel on it until the bleeding stopped. She didn't even lecture him, knowing by his muffled sobs that it wasn't necessary. She just held him on her lap as she sat on the side of the tub and rocked him gently.

His thoughts came back to the present, and he listened to the night. He heard every sound that drifted through the open window by his bed. It was like being suddenly struck blind and seeing the world through his ears alone. At first he just let them flow indiscriminately through him as they intertwined and blended together. Then he began to differentiate, concentrating on each sound individually, isolating it and filtering out everything else until it alone remained.

The barking dog, he decided, was the small terrier that belonged to the Cassidys. They were a young couple with an energetic toddler Josh baby-sat for from time to time. The child spent a large part of his day monotonously chasing the little dog around the fenced backyard. Each stiff-legged step was accented by his constant repetitious call of "Dog-dog-dog-dog" as he ran precariously along, his arms outstretched. The terrier always managed to stay one step ahead of the child, just out of his insistent grasp. It kept life interesting for the boy but made it miserable for the dog, who had grown increasingly high-strung and nervous.

The frogs resided in the small pond the Morrisons had dug next to their garden. The retired couple had lived in the same house all their married life. He had worked his way up through middle management at the local bank, while she had tirelessly donated her time to civic projects and church functions.

A few years ago Mr. Morrison misplaced a client's loan application. He knew it was in his office somewhere but couldn't for the life of him find it. Eventually he had to have his secretary retype it so he could complete the transaction. A few weeks later he spent hours searching for a payroll deposit that he had picked up for a local business on his way to work. It turned up in the bottom drawer of a filing cabinet that he never used, and he began to wonder if someone in the bank was playing tricks on him.

Similar incidents piled up, and he began to have trouble remembering customers' names that he had known for years. Then he started showing up for work at odd hours, and his usually neat appearance slowly deteriorated. He looked disheveled, forgetting to shave, his clothes rumpled and stained. He would sit at his desk for hours, staring out the window, a lost look in his eyes.

His secretary called and talked to his wife. She too had noticed changes in his behavior at home, though she hadn't given it much thought. His wife talked him into setting up an appointment for a routine checkup, then called the doctor while he was at work and laid the cards out on the table. The tests came back, and he was diagnosed with Alzheimer's. They were devastated.

He took early retirement from the bank, and they had a big farewell party for him after work on a Friday in the fall. At first his co-workers and friends dropped by regularly for a drink and to talk about old times, but after a while the visits became less and less frequent. He spent much of his time puttering around the house or working in the garden. He had good days and bad days. Days when he was the man he had always been and the world looked clear and bright, and days when he saw everything through a fog, not sure who or where he was. More and more he wandered off and had to be led back home by a neighbor or the police—who knew him now on a first-name basis.

Gradually the bad days began to outnumber the good ones until they were almost all he had left. His wife stayed home and looked after him every day but Wednesdays, when a nurse came in so she could go into town to shop or visit with old friends she rarely saw anymore.

Josh continued filtering out the sounds one by one, assigning each a place and a history until only one was left. It was a low, muffled sound that he couldn't quite place. Holding his breath, he listened carefully, but still it eluded him. He sat up in bed and put his ear to the open window, but it didn't grow any louder or more distinct. Finally he got up and quietly opened the door to his room. He walked down the hall, his bare feet silent on the hardwood floor. The sound led him to the closed door of his mother's bedroom, and he stood motionless in front of it, listening. He knocked lightly, and it stopped.

He waited, then called softly.

"Mom?"

The seconds ticked by.

"Mom?" he called again.

"Yes," she finally answered.

He opened the door. In the dim light from the open window he could see her silhouette lying curled up on the bed. He took a step toward her, then stopped.

"Are you all right?" he asked.

"I'm fine," she said with a quaver in her voice.

"You don't sound fine," he said, moving to sit on the side of the bed.

She didn't reply, only sniffed and wiped her eyes with the palm of her hand while he waited.

"What's the matter?" he asked, reaching out and touching her shoulder.

"Nothing," she said hollowly. "It's just...nothing."

"I've never seen you cry over 'nothing' before. What is it?" he asked again.

There was a long pause.

"It's silly, really," she said, sniffing loudly and sitting up in bed. "I couldn't sleep, so I was just lying here thinking about tomorrow.

Planning what we would have for your graduation dinner when Aunt Betty is here." She started to cry quietly again. "One thing led to another, and it occurred to me what tomorrow means."

Her tears fell steadily now, and she put her head in her hands. Josh patted her shoulder and waited, letting her take her time. Finally she breathed in deeply, composed herself, and continued.

"Tomorrow means that you'll be leaving me."

"I'm not going anywhere," Josh protested.

"Oh, maybe not for a while, but it'll happen. It has to happen. Maybe it'll be gradual at first. You'll come by every day to see me and sometimes even stay for dinner. Then after a while it'll be every other day, and one day I'll look up and you'll be gone."

She reached over to the bedside table and took several tissues from the box and blew her nose.

"But I won't—"

She reached out and gripped his arm firmly, looking him in the eye. "It's okay, it's supposed to be this way. It's all in the big plan, birds leaving the nest and all that. God knows I want you to go out and find your place in the world. It's just that..." she hesitated.

"What?"

"It's just that all of a sudden it hit me. Here I am, my life half over, everything about me sagging or turning gray, my job is the pits, I haven't met a man in years that I would even consider going out with, there's never enough money..." She paused and sighed. "And soon I'll be doing all of it alone. Without you—the one really important thing I've had in my life."

She reached over, put her arms around him, and held him tight.

"My life hasn't turned out like I thought it would, Josh," she said, letting go of him. "It's not supposed to be like this. You're supposed to have someone you love to grow old with. I guess I'm just scared of what the future might bring."

"I'm scared, too," Josh said. "I have to go out there alone and figure out what I'm supposed to do with my life."

"I know, but you're young. I've already missed my chance, and they don't come around but once."

Josh got off the bed and looked out the window into the darkness, then turned back to face her.

"You talk as though your life is over, but it's not. Things will get better. Someone will come along, and no matter what you say I'll always be here for you."

"I know you will," she said, blowing her nose again. "I didn't mean to spoil your day. I'm very proud of you, Josh. You've had to put up with a lot in your life, and you've always made the best of it."

He got back on the bed and they lay side by side in the darkness, just as they used to when he had a bad dream.

"We've had some good times, too," Josh said

hopefully. "Like the time we just took off after Christmas and drove to Florida. I remember you said that you wanted to leave the gloomy weather behind and go somewhere that was sunny and nice, somewhere there weren't lines of rude people waiting with presents to return. We drove all night until we got to Key West and couldn't go any farther. You took me through Hemingway's house, and we ate all the boiled shrimp you could eat at a restaurant overlooking the water."

"Papa's."

"What?"

"That was the name of the restaurant. I never dreamed you could eat so much," she said, and laughed. "I think you almost put them out of business."

"I remember you gave me a quarter, and I played a Jimmy Buffett song on the jukebox while we watched the sun set over the water. It was the best time I've ever had."

They lay there thinking back over all they had shared, and soon they both drifted off to sleep. The room brightened as the full moon rose over the trees, shining down on them through the bedroom window. Outside, the neighbor's dog barked again, and the frogs continued their moonlight serenade. But they slept peacefully through it all, as the earth slowly turned toward the start of another day.

Chapter 21

Turning Point

The three boys sat at a picnic table under the pavilion in the state park, staring out at the flat expanse of water. The waves of last weekend had dissipated as quickly as they had formed, leaving the usually placid gulf behind. It was Thursday, and the beach was deserted. The crowds didn't arrive until the weekend in the off-season, but once school was out every day would be packed.

The noon air was still. It left a glassy sheen on the water that reflected the sky, blurring the line between them until they appeared as one seamless backdrop. Against this smooth canvas the slightest imperfection was revealed, and they watched as ripples from a school of baitfish played across the surface.

"Well, it's finally here," Josh said and took a swallow of lukewarm Coke.

Their eyes swiveled in unison as a mullet jumped near shore.

"It's felt like Christmas Eve for weeks now," he continued. "You know how when you were a kid it seemed to take forever for morning to arrive?"

"Yeah," Chris said, thinking back. "I'd lie there awake for hours, staring at the ceiling, my mind buzzing like electricity was running through it."

"I would tell myself just to go to sleep, and it would be here before I know it," Josh said.

"But it never worked," Mark added, finishing his thought. "I'd lie there and lie there—"

"The clock would tick and a floorboard would creak. I never knew the night was so long," Josh said, pulling his knees up against his chest and staring out to sea. "Then I would close my eyes just for a minute, and when I opened them again it had happened. And at the foot of my bed, the stocking that looked so limp and sad only a second before was bulging—"

"With candy and fruit," Chris broke in, "a top, a paddle ball—"

"A harmonica, a comic book, and a magic set," Mark said, finishing the list.

"Then it was over," Josh said. "I would sit and stare at my presents, everything I had hoped and dreamed for spread out in front of me. But I still had an empty feeling deep inside, like something was missing."

He leaned his head back and looked up at the pavilion's ceiling, which was riddled with dirt dauber nests.

"I don't know whether to be happy or sad," Chris said. "I mean, it's kind of scary."

"Everybody will be going different directions," Josh added. "We'll probably never see most of them again."

No one spoke for a minute. Today was a turning point, marked by the simple passing of a piece of paper.

"Made any plans yet?" Mark asked, looking over at Josh.

"Well, my mom got me on at the store for the summer," he replied. "I'll be filling in for the regulars when they take their vacations."

"What about in the fall?" Chris asked.

"I'm not sure," Josh said slowly. "I'd like to go to college, but unless something comes up...I don't know."

They lapsed into silence again. The sun beat down on the sand, distorting the air in front of them. A drop of sweat formed on Josh's temple, reached critical mass, and streaked down the side of his face.

"Man, it's hot," he said, wiping off his face on his shirtsleeve. "I think I'll take a swim, then head home."

"I'll pass," Chris said.

"I'm out, too," Mark agreed, spreading out on the picnic table and closing his eyes. The bandages on his forehead and leg were the only visible reminders of last weekend.

Josh slipped off his shirt and shoes and started for the water. Halfway there he realized that he had miscalculated the temperature of the sand and picked up his pace. He ran straight into the water, his momentum carrying him until he toppled forward and dove into the tranquil sea.

He flipped over on his back and swam gracefully out until the water was over his head. The sun blazed down, and when he looked back, his friends were almost invisible under the shadow of the pavilion. He rolled over and swam forward on his chest, then jackknifed and dove, his feet pointing to the sky. The water grew cold and dark as he neared the sandy bottom. Swimming just above the sea floor, he spotted a half-buried sand dollar and reached down to pick it up. It was the size of a quarter and brittle as a eggshell. He pushed off the bottom and shot upward, feeling the water grow warmer and the light brighter. His lungs ached, and just when he felt that he couldn't last any longer, he broke through the surface and breathed in deeply. After swimming leisurely to shore, he jogged back up to the shade of the pavilion.

"I got you something while I was out," he said, dropping the sand dollar in Chris's upturned hand and drying himself with a towel. Mark snored peacefully on the table behind them.

"Thanks, I'll put it in my savings account," Chris said sarcastically as he absently turned it over and over in his hand. "I've been thinking," he said, staring straight ahead of him. "Things aren't ever going to be the same again, are they."

It wasn't really a question, rather something he had worked out on his own that needed confirmation.

"What do you mean?" Josh asked, sitting next to him.

"You know—us, the Three Musketeers. Riding waves at the jetty, hanging out at lunch and flipping peas at each other. After tonight everything will be different," he said, looking down at the sand dollar.

"No," Josh answered. "Things aren't going

to be the same, but that isn't always a bad thing."

"You think so?" Chris asked hopefully, turning to look at him.

"Sure. Change is the only thing that you can really count on. Take today," he said, nodding at the calm water. "It's days like this that make the waves seem even better." He stood up and put on his shirt. "Wake up sleepyhead," he said, poking Mark. "It's showtime."

Chapter 22

A Single Step

Even though the sun had gone down outside, the gymnasium was almost as hot as the beach had been at noon. Exhaust fans in the ceiling provided a little relief, but they had been turned off before the program began so the speakers could be heard. Josh sat in his cap and gown in the stifling heat, surrounded by his classmates.

Mr. Howell, the high school principal, introduced the speaker, a local judge of some repute. His gown covered his massive frame like a tent, and perspiration ran down his face. As he spoke, he mopped at it periodically with a soggy handkerchief.

It was the standard speech about incorporating the values they had learned from their parents and teachers into their lives. Josh had heard him give the same one at graduation a few years ago and had a hard time concentrating on it now. Instead he scanned the gym, searching for his father's face in the crowd. His robe stuck to him as he squirmed in the hard metal folding chair. He felt a little light-headed from the heat, and the air seemed to pulse as the judge's words boomed out through the PA system.

Josh's mind began to drift, and he thought about Mr. Davis. Stories poured out of him as effortlessly as water from a spring, but he noticed that they always seemed to have a point. He began to wonder if there was more to his job than just recording an old man's memories.

Applause broke out around him, and his attention was brought back to the stage. The judge gave a nod of acknowledgment, and Mr. Howell returned to the podium.

"Thank you for that inspiring talk, Judge. I'm sure the students will take your words with them as they leave here today. And now our salutatorian, Megan Hall, will honor us with a few words."

Megan sat in front of Josh in English class. She was Miss Everything at school: head cheerleader, president of the senior class, and editor of the school paper. As well as being smart and outgoing, she was pretty to a fault, and the extreme heat didn't seem to have affected her at all. She gave the audience a warm smile and began her speech.

"As we, the senior class of 1989, leave here today, we will take with us many fond memories of the time we have spent together...."

He glanced over at Mark, sitting two rows away. He had dozed off, and Josh envied the ease with which he seemed to have put the events of last weekend behind him. Chris was sitting on the far end, listening attentively to the speech, though Josh wondered if it was the speech or Megan that held his attention.

". . . and no matter how far we may travel," she continued, "our time here will always be close to our hearts. Thank you." She smiled broadly as the crowd broke into applause.

"That was a lovely speech, Megan," the principal said as he returned to the lectern. "I think we all would do well to follow your example." He looked down at the program in front of him. "Our valedictorian this year is David Thornton, who will share his thoughts with us."

Josh didn't know David very well because he was in all AP courses. Rumor had it that when a question came up in class that the teacher wasn't sure of, all eyes immediately turned to David. He walked slowly to the center of the stage, put his hands on each side of the podium, and looked down at the seniors. With their robes on, they must have appeared as disembodied heads floating on a calm blue sea. David stopped at each individual face, and Josh felt himself blush when he looked his way. It was disconcerting, like a minister or salesman whose eye contact lasted a bit too long. The audience began to grow restless, shifting in their seats and fanning themselves with their programs. Finally David turned and spoke to the crowd in a clear voice.

"What is truth?"

There was another long pause, and the audience looked nervously at one another. There was something disturbing about the question, especially the way it was thrown out across the room as if it demanded an answer.

"This is a question that I was asked once in an interview, and I admit that it caught me off guard. However, I've thought about it a lot since then, and I believe that I have developed a satisfactory answer.

"Truth, in the form of thoughts and ideas, does not exist."

A buzz of whispered voices ran through the crowd, and David waited patiently until it had died down before continuing.

"Nobel Prize–winning author Hermann Hesse wrote in his novel *Siddhartha* that 'in every truth the opposite is equally true. For example, a truth can only be expressed and enveloped in words if it is one-sided. Everything that is thought and expressed in words *is* one-sided, only half the truth; it all lacks totality, completeness, unity.'

"In *The Sirens of Titan*, Kurt Vonnegut penned a fitting analogy on truth and the equal validity of opposites. Vonnegut wrote: 'Just imagine that your Daddy is the smartest man who ever lived on Earth, and he knows everything there is to find out, and he is exactly right about everything, and he can prove he is right about everything. Now imagine another little child on some nice world a million light years away, and that little child's Daddy is the smartest man who ever lived on that nice world so far away. And he is just as smart and just as right as your Daddy is. Both Daddies are smart, and both Daddies are right. Only if they ever met each other they would get into a terrible argument, because they wouldn't agree on anything.' Vonnegut goes on to explain, 'The reason both Daddies can be right and still get into terrible fights is because there are so many different ways of being right.' "

He paused again to let the words sink in.

"It is important to be open-minded and understand that no individual, no single political party, and no one religion possesses the truth. The belief that any one entity *can* possess the truth is what leads to humanity's suffering. In the last century alone, the Holocaust, the cold war, and the ongoing conflict in Israel are examples on a large scale of the terrible argument that would ensue if the two 'Daddies' from different worlds ever met. These confrontations occur because each side believes that it alone holds the truth. What an egotistical assumption.

"I would like to impress on my fellow classmates the importance of keeping an open mind throughout life. When we are able to accept the fact that Buddhism's two hundred and fifty million followers are just as right in their beliefs as Christians are in theirs, then we have begun to listen to what Hesse told us in 1922: that 'in every truth the opposite is equally true.' And when we accept this teaching and realize that we possess no more or less truth than anyone else in the world, then—and only then—will we experience a more peaceful existence on this earth."

There was total silence in the gym. David stared out over the sea of faces, and a faint smile played over his lips as they stared back at him uneasily. Tentative applause broke out, spread politely, then died quickly.

The principal cleared his throat. "Well, David, I'm sure you've given us all something to think about," he said diplomatically.

It was time for the presentation of diplomas, and all the seniors rose and walked toward the stage in single file. As each name was called, Mr. Howell handed the student a diploma and shook their hand while the line advanced slowly.

"John Wilcox Aldridge."

The line moved a step closer.

"James Allen Alexander."

Josh stared intently at the back of the head of the girl in front of him.

"Mary Reynolds Barton."

He was next.

"Joshua Armstrong Bell."

Josh stepped forward and shook the principal's hand as he received his diploma, then he was walking down the aisle and out the door of the gym. He waited for Mark and Chris, and together they walked down the hall to the reception in the library.

Josh moved slowly through the crowd of parents and graduates, still looking for his father. Instead he saw his mother and aunt standing together, sipping punch, and gave them both a hug.

"Have you seen Dad?" he asked.

"No," his mother replied. "I thought he might be with you."

Josh shook his head and continued to scan the crowd.

"Let me get a picture of the graduate with his favorite aunt," Mrs. Bell said as she fumbled through her purse for the camera.

Josh put his arm around Aunt Betty and managed a smile as the flash went off. Over his mother's shoulder, through the spots still swimming before his eyes, he saw Mr. Davis walking toward them. The old man didn't say anything about coming, and Josh hadn't expected to see him here. Dressed in a coat and tie, with his white hair combed neatly, he looked the epitome of a southern gentleman.

"Congratulations," he said, shaking Josh's hand. He handed him a package wrapped in white paper.

"Thank you," Josh said, still recovering from the surprise of seeing him. His mother nudged him, and he quickly added, "I believe you've met my mother, Mr. Davis, and this is my aunt."

"I've enjoyed getting to know your son, Mrs. Bell. He's a fine young man," Mr. Davis told her as he shook hands with each of them.

"You'll get no arguments from me," she said, putting her arm around Josh's waist. "Let me get a picture of you and Josh together," she suggested.

They stood stiffly side by side while she took the photograph.

"Well, I must be going," Mr. Davis said after another minute of small talk. "It's a long way out to my house in the dark, and my driving isn't what it used to be."

"Sure," Josh said. "And thanks," he added, holding up the present.

"I'm mighty proud of you, son," he said, patting Josh on the arm.

Before Josh could reply, he had turned and walked away.

"Who was that again?" Aunt Betty asked.

"Someone I deliver meals to," Josh answered, momentarily taking his eyes off the receding back. "He lives on the bay, and I've been staying and working for him every afternoon," he added. When he looked back, the old man had disappeared.

Later, in his room, Josh unwrapped his present. Inside was a book called A River Runs Through It by Norman Maclean. He opened it to the title page and read the inscription in Mr. Davis's hand:

Josh,

A wise man once said that a journey of a thousand miles begins with a single step. Let tonight be the beginning—not the end—of your journey down the road to knowledge and wisdom.

Sincerely,
William Davis

He undressed and lay on his bed, thinking about the day. Everything whirled around in his head: the beach, the hot gym, David's speech, and walking up on the stage to get his diploma. He thought about Mr. Davis showing up unexpectedly, and his father, who had let him down again.

Josh opened the book to the first page and began to read about a world far removed from his own. The beaches, tourists, and surfboards that he knew so well were replaced by woods, streams, and trout fishing. He felt the natural rhythm of the words as they described a time and place long past, sweeping him up in the story about another shattered family.

He read on long into the night, until he had turned the last page and read the final words:

Of course, now I am too old to be much of a fisherman, and now of course I usually fish the big waters alone, although some friends think I shouldn't. Like many fly fishermen in western Montana where the summer days are almost Arctic in length, I often do not start fishing until the cool of the evening. Then in the Arctic half-light of the canyon, all existence fades to a being with my soul and memories and the sounds of the Big Blackfoot River and a four-count rhythm and the hope that a fish will rise.

Eventually, all things merge into one, and a river runs through it. The river was cut by the world's great flood and runs over rocks from the basement of time. On some of the rocks are timeless raindrops. Under the rocks are the words, and some of the words are theirs.

I am haunted by waters.

Josh closed the book and sat in his own dim circle of light, cast by the lamp beside his bed. He thought again of Mr. Davis and saw in him the same bittersweet love of the world.

Turning out the light, he closed his eyes. The house was quiet, and as he drifted off to sleep, the words wove their way in and out of his consciousness: "A journey of a thousand miles begins with a single step."

Chapter 23

Fading Images

Josh opened his eyes with a start. It had seemed so real, he thought as he tried to pull the jumbled images of his dream back into sharper focus. He looked around his room, but everything seemed the same: the bluebird sat in its cage, and his surfboard still leaned against the wall in the corner.

He closed his eyes again and concentrated, but already the dream had started to fade. What made so much sense only a minute ago was now blurred and dim. It was something about searching for his father at the graduation reception last night.

As he prodded his memory, it started to come back to him. He could see his father's back disappearing through the crowd in front of him but could never quite catch up. He wandered through the room, weaving his way until he found his father standing alone in a corner, reading a book off the library shelf. He walked up behind him and put his hand on his shoulder. His father turned, but as Josh watched, his features began to dissolve and rearrange. Wrinkles spread out over his face, and his hair turned white. When he looked up from his book, Josh realized that he was staring into the eyes of the old man.

Mr. Davis was sitting on the porch when Josh arrived at his house that afternoon. It was another scorcher, but the heat was tempered somewhat by the paddle fan that churned the air above them and the iced tea that left puddles of sweat on the table.

"Well, now that graduation is over, what are your plans?" Mr. Davis asked as he rocked slowly back and forth.

"I've got a job for the summer at the discount store," Josh told him.

"That's not what I meant," he said. "Have you given any thought to what we talked about?"

Josh sighed. "I just don't think college is going to happen," he said.

Mr. Davis didn't say anything.

"Thanks for the book," Josh told him, changing the subject. "I really enjoyed it."

"You've read it already?" Mr. Davis replied, raising an eyebrow. "I just gave it to you last night."

"I started it and couldn't put it down," Josh said.

"I thought you might like it because Norman Maclean was struggling with the same question that you're dealing with."

"Me?" Josh said.

"I could see it in your story. It's something everyone asks at one time or another," the old man said. "Is it worth it." He looked Josh in the eye. "Love isn't easy in the best of times, and when things go wrong it's like someone is reaching inside your chest and squeezing your heart. You can't love without pain, Josh. If you care for someone, it's going to hurt. That's what your story and Norman Maclean's are really about."

"He didn't even bother to come last night," Josh said, looking away

"That doesn't change anything; he's still your father. It's a bond that's hard to break. My son and I went through a rough time, too. For years it seemed like nothing either of us did ever turned out right. Then Mary got sick...."

He opened the door to the hospital room quietly, so as not to disturb her if she were sleeping. She was lying on her back in the elevated bed, watching the birds in the sycamore tree outside her window. She saw his reflection in the glass and turned, and he looked at her once beautiful face that was now pinched and thin.

He lowered his eyes and looked at the gaunt hand with the hospital bracelet on it. Each time he came, he forgot to prepare himself for the change the last few months had brought. He tried not to show it, but she had always been able to see right through him, and her face dropped at the thought of the pain she was causing him. Then her eyes grew wide as she saw what he held loosely in his hands.

"Oh, Will!" she said. "They're lovely."

He looked down at the bouquet of flowers that he had forgotten he held.

"They're from the garden," he said. "Everything we planted is blooming now."

He stuck his hand out as awkwardly as a boy on a first date and handed them to her. She pressed them to her face and breathed in deeply.

"They smell wonderful," she said, "just like spring." Her eyes began to water, and she turned away. "Put them in water for me."

He filled the empty vase at the bathroom sink and dropped the flowers into it, fumbling as he tried to arrange them.

"Bring them here," she said, shaking her head.

He brought the vase over to the bed and helped her sit up.

"I saw Dr. Ross this morning," he said while she worked on the flowers. "I told him what we talked about, and he agreed."

"You mean I can go home?" she asked, looking up at him, a note of hope creeping into her voice.

"Whenever you feel up to it."

"I want to leave today," she said firmly. "I don't want to spend another night here if I can help it."

"I'll see what I can do."

It hadn't been easy, but by late afternoon the paperwork was completed and the nurse was wheeling her through the lobby to the car waiting at the entrance. Mr. Davis walked behind them, trying to keep up.

"We're gonna miss you," the nurse told

her as Mr. Davis opened the passenger-side door and they helped her inside.

"I can't say that I'm going to miss this place," she replied, looking up at the cold concrete building, "but you've been good to me, and I'll miss you, too."

The nurse closed the car door, and they drove slowly away.

"Let's take the long way home, Will," she said.

He looked over at her to see how she was holding up, then nodded and turned onto the winding two-lane road that followed the bay. They pulled up the drive to their house, and he helped her up the back steps.

"I think I need to take a little rest," she said weakly.

He helped her to the bedroom and into the big four-poster bed that they had shared for over fifty years now. He made a fuss of arranging the pillows, then lay down next to her and watched her sleep.

The next few weeks passed quietly, and she seemed to blossom like the flowers he had planted outside her bedroom window. He kept up with the numerous medications, arranging the pills by her place at the table and making sure that she took them all. She would sit in a folding chair outside for hours, watching him work in the garden or looking out over the bay. He began to forget what the doctors had said and started to feel that the hospital had been only a bad dream. Then one morning she didn't come to breakfast. He went in the bedroom to check on her and found her still in bed. He sat beside her, and her eyes opened when she felt his presence.

"Aren't you coming to breakfast?" he asked, concern creeping into his voice.

"I'm just not feeling like it today," she said tiredly. "Why don't you start without me."

He sat at the kitchen table in silence, eating halfheartedly and realizing for the first time what life would be like without her.

The days passed slowly, but there was no joy left in them. She grew weaker and weaker, until the big double bed and the window next to it marked the boundaries of her world.

One morning early in July when she was asleep, he picked up the telephone in the kitchen and dialed the number. He had dialed it many other mornings as well but had always hung up before the first ring. This time he fought off the urge to press the button that would sever the connection. It was picked up on the fourth ring.

"Hello," said the voice on the other end of the line, the voice that he had not heard in years.

He started to speak the words he had rehearsed so many times but was interrupted.

"I'm not in right now, but if you'll leave a message after the tone, I'll get back to you as soon as possible."

He started to hang up, but since he had come this far he decided not to turn back now.

"Son," he said evenly, "I know that—"

There was a loud beep that stopped him in his tracks, and he started over again.

"Son, your mother is very sick." He hesitated, trying to decide how much to tell him. "I don't think she has much time left." He felt his voice tighten and swallowed hard to push down the mixture of pain and pride. "I know that we haven't seen eye to eye in the past, but I think you should come home and be with her while you still can."

He hung up the phone. It felt strange to pour out his heart to a machine, but maybe it was best this way. He remembered back to the happy little boy he used to take fishing. Then his mind jumped ahead to the stranger they had greeted when he'd returned from Vietnam, bitter and angry at the world for what he had seen and done. They had tried to return to the way it was before, but it just hadn't worked, and their only child had drifted away from them. Even though time had healed some of the wounds, they hadn't seen each other in years.

The memory faded, and he realized that he was standing on the end of the wharf. He didn't even remember leaving the house, but he must have. He slumped into one of the chairs, and felt very much alone for the first time he could remember. Staring at the gray line of the horizon in the distance, he thought about the son he never saw, separated by more than the miles between them. Then he looked up at the bedroom window and thought of Mary, preparing for a journey of her own.

She grew weaker through the night, tossing and turning in her sleep. He sat by her side and held her hand until dawn, when he stood—

his back cramped and sore—to stare out the window at the morning light. She sensed the change and opened her eyes, looking at his profile against the glass.

"Will?" she said softly.

He turned at her voice and sat down next to her.

"It's not going to be easy for you," she said thoughtfully, "but I want you to promise me that you won't give up."

He didn't say anything for a moment, then nodded. "I'll try," he said brokenly.

There was the sound of a car in the drive, and he went to the back door. He opened it just as the man standing there was about to knock. Even with the intervening years he could still see the boy in him.

"I came as soon as I could," his son whispered. "How is she?"

"She's very weak. I don't think she can last much longer," he said, trying to keep his voice strong.

The old man led him back to the bedroom and stood aside so he could enter first.

"Who was it, Will?" she asked, her face turned toward the window.

Without saying a word, he crossed the room in two strides and leaned over the bed. He held her tightly, and she gripped him as though she would never let go.

They sat with her all through the day, and she seemed better than she had been in weeks. But as the sun began to drop over the horizon, so did her spirits, and through the long night she faded slowly like a wilting flower. As the sun rose on another day, she drew a ragged breath, and they both felt it slowly leave her body for the last time.

He took it hard, harder than he could have imagined. He lay awake at night in the big empty bed, staring at the ceiling and listening to the ticking of the clock and the creaking of the old house. He thought back over the times they had spent together, trying to burn each moment forever in his memory. The hours would pass slowly, second by second, memory by memory, until dawn finally broke, and he would rise to face another day.

After the funeral was over and everyone else had left, they sat together at the kitchen table. The old man looked at the packed bags standing by the back door but still couldn't find the right words. As his son stood up to leave, he knew that it was now or never.

"Son," he said, not knowing quite how to begin. "You've lost a mother, and I've lost a wife. It's left a big hole in each of our lives that we're not ever going to fill, but we still have each other, and I don't want to lose that again."

His son stood still for a moment, then reached out to his father as the years of bitterness between them melted away.

"I know it's hard," Mr. Davis said, looking over at Josh. "But even with the pain, it's worth every minute of it."

Josh closed the notebook and nodded thoughtfully.

"Can you be here early tomorrow?" Mr. Davis asked. "I've got something I want to do."

"Sure," Josh said.

"Good, I'll see you then."

He watched the boy drive away, then settled back into his rocker. He glanced at the empty chair across from him, and for an instant he saw her indelible image still sitting in it.

"It is worth it," he said aloud to her as the image faded gradually away.

Chapter 24

⁓

Destiny

W hen Josh arrived in the morning, Mr. Davis was sitting in his chair on the end of the wharf. The old man waved, and Josh walked out to join him.

"You came at a good time," Mr. Davis remarked when he walked up.

"Why's that?"

"I was trying to splice this line together, but I'm not having much luck," he said, flexing his stiff fingers. "I thought you might lend me a hand, so to speak."

"Sure," Josh replied, dropping his notebook on the dock and pulling up a chair next to him. "What do I do?"

"Well, you can start by separating these strands." He handed Josh the two pieces of rope. "In my day when something broke you fixed it," he said, watching Josh work. "That's right, now you have to work the two pieces together. This one goes through first."

"Like this?" Josh asked.

"No, over the top." He watched Josh weave the two pieces together. "You catch on quick, son," he said as Josh got the hang of it. "Because of the way they're made, you can't even do this with most ropes today."

"But I'll bet the new ones last longer, so you probably don't need to," Josh commented.

"True. The old ropes didn't last forever, and you had to take care of them, hanging them out to dry and coiling them up neatly when you were through. But maybe learning how to take care of something is part of what's missing today. Now everything is just stamped out at a factory and thrown away as soon as the shine wears off," he said, showing Josh how to finish making the splice.

"Take that little boat over there," he continued, nodding at the sailboat that floated in the previously empty boathouse. "I got her for my tenth birthday. She was made by a little boatyard in Mobile, and the foreman sailed over here himself to deliver her." He gazed affectionately at the small boat.

"They made her from good solid wood planking, not a bit of plywood or fiberglass in her. She's held up well over the years, but I had to take care of her, too. I named her *Destiny*."

Josh smiled. "That's kind of a big name for a little boat," he said.

Mr. Davis shrugged. "I was just a boy at the time, what did I know."

"Is this the boat you were in when you caught the tarpon?" Josh asked.

"The very same one. My best friend and I spent most of our childhood sailing her. Then, after I left home, my father took her out of the water and put her in the storage shed. This is the first time I've had her in the water since I moved back here," he said. "There was a time when I was too young to take her out by myself; now I'm too old." He stared at the boat, then looked over at Josh. "But I thought you might help me with her one last time."

"Sure," Josh agreed.

"Well, let's go," he said, getting up.

"But I've never been sailing," Josh said, reconsidering as he looked at the frail figure standing before him.

"Well, then you're in for a real treat, my boy," Mr. Davis said. "There's nothing quite like the wind at your back and the open water before you."

With the old man's supervision, Josh maneuvered the boat out of the stall and tied it up to the dock. He climbed aboard, and Mr. Davis told him how to rig the lines from the wharf.

"No, not that way—through the other end,

that's right. Now, pass the line through the pulleys on the boom, and raise the sails."

Soon they were ready, and Josh helped him into the boat. It was a slow process, the old man's body protesting every move.

When he was finally seated behind the tiller, Mr. Davis cut a regal figure. His broad-brimmed hat was pulled down low against the wind, and his khaki shirt and pants were close enough to a sailor's whites to draw comparisons. He held the tiller firm and steady, as if it had only been days since he was last out on the water.

They cast off from the dock and Mr. Davis pulled in the mainsheet, filling the sail. The pier slid away behind them as the boat picked up speed, and they headed out into the open bay. As they cleared the point, a gust of wind heeled the boat over sharply.

"Move over here," Mr. Davis said, indicating the spot next to him.

Josh obligingly switched sides, and *Destiny* leveled off.

"Always sit on the windward side of the boat to balance the pull of the sails," he explained.

Billowing clouds were pushed across the sky by the southerly breeze as the boat continued out into the bay on a tight tack into the wind. It cut cleanly through the water as the chop bounced off her bow. When he looked back, Josh was amazed to see the dock far behind them and growing smaller every minute.

"Coming about!" Mr. Davis called as he

swung the tiller over hard. "Uncleat the jib for me, son," he said, pointing to it, "and secure it on the other side."

The boat turned into the wind, and Josh ducked as the boom swung past. Then the sails filled again as they headed out on a new tack.

"Want to try your hand at the tiller?" Mr. Davis asked.

"I guess so, if you'll show me what to do," Josh said.

They changed places, and his hand replaced the old man's at the helm.

"Just keep her steady," Mr. Davis said. "If the wind gusts and we heel over, turn us into the wind or let out on the mainsheet and she'll right herself."

Josh nodded, but everything was happening a little too fast to take it in all at once.

"Remember that the tiller works the opposite of what you might think," he continued. "When you push it to starboard, the bow will turn to port."

"Which way is starboard?" Josh asked, confused.

"Starboard is to the right, and port the left."

"Well, why don't you just say left and right?"

"To confuse the landlubbers," Mr. Davis whispered confidentially.

Josh experimented, making small turns to try to get the feel of it. He turned the boat tighter into the wind and saw how the sails started to luff as the boat slowed. Then he pushed the tiller the other way and felt them fill again as she surged forward.

Just then a gust of wind hit, and they heeled far over to the side. Instinctively Josh pulled the tiller toward him, causing the boat to tilt even farther.

"No, son! The other way!" the old man yelled.

Frozen, Josh kept an iron grip on the tiller, and *Destiny* leaned precariously on her side. Mr. Davis reached over, popped the mainsheet out of the jam cleat, and let go of it. The line whistled through the pulleys as the sail swung out into the wind, and the boat quickly righted itself.

"I—I'm sorry," the boy stammered.

"That's all right," Mr. Davis said. "Every novice has to make that mistake at least once. Remember, if she leans over too far, just let go."

"Yes, sir."

"Now, give it another try. You almost had the hang of it."

The old man pulled in the mainsheet, and they started forward again, quickly picking up speed.

"Notice the way the wind looks on the water," he said. "You can see a gust coming a long way off by the ripples it makes."

He pointed to a steadily approaching patch of rougher water.

"See it coming? Now you're ready when it gets here."

The boat heeled over again, but this time Josh turned the tiller to compensate.

"That's it. I think you've got it now."

Josh grinned at the compliment. Ahead they noticed a school of dolphins, their fins rolling through the water.

"Thar she blows, lad," Mr. Davis said in a thick seaman's accent. "Steer us for 'em."

Josh angled the boat so that their paths would intersect, and they grew steadily closer.

"*Destiny* is gaining on 'em, my boy," the old man said with a chuckle.

They cut through the school, and a dolphin surfaced next to the boat. Air whistled out of its blowhole as it looked up at them.

"Ahoy there!" Mr. Davis called. "Seen any mullet around here?"

His question was answered by a shower of spray that cascaded over them as the dolphin dove, slapping the water with its tail. Josh laughed as the old man sputtered, taking off his hat and wringing it out over the side.

"Well, that's a rude reply if I've ever seen one," Mr. Davis said, wiping his face on his sleeve. "They say they have saved sailors from drowning at sea, but I'm beginning to have my doubts."

"I've heard that, too," Josh said. "But when I'm surfing, they always seem to keep their distance."

"Maybe they know you don't need saving," he replied. "They're probably the smartest creatures on earth except for man, and to tell you the truth, I'm not that sure about man."

The sun began to go down, and the breeze started to die. They turned for home, running easily with the wind. After an hour of milking the remains of the breeze, they slid gently up to the dock—their sails lifeless. Josh helped Mr. Davis out of the boat, and the old man lowered himself into his chair with a sigh.

"Yes sir, *Destiny* and I have had some good times together. She's been all you could ask for in a boat," he said as Josh lowered the sails. "Sailing can give you whatever you're looking for," he continued. "Adventure when the wind is up and the clouds are racing across the sky, or serenity when only a gentle breeze is blowing and the sun is setting in the west."

A flock of pelicans appeared, swooping low over the water to glide for a seemingly endless amount of time just above the surface, then flapping their wings in unison to regain their momentum. Josh secured the boat in its stall and picked up his notebook where he had left it, then sat next to the old man.

"That's one of the most beautiful sights there is," he said, nodding at the birds. "And to think that only a few years ago they had almost disappeared."

Josh watched as the pelicans rounded the point and vanished from sight.

"I remember one time in particular," Mr. Davis said as Josh opened the notebook. "It was in the summer of my twelfth year, and I was dying to do something adventurous. John and I had been planning a trip to the old fort at the mouth of the bay for months now, and the time was finally ripe to spring it on our parents...."

"I don't know, Will. Maybe when you're a little older," his mother said as she wiped a cloth across the kitchen table.

"But we've been out all day before. It'll be just like that, only longer."

"A lot can happen—"

"We'll be real careful. It's not that far to the fort. We can make it in a day, easy."

"But what if a storm comes up?"

"We haven't had a big one in years," Will said, ready for this tack.

"Well, then we're due for one anytime now," she told him.

"*Please*, Mother?" he said, looking as forlorn as he could.

"What did John's parents say?" she asked, putting down the cloth and turning to face him with her hands on her hips.

"They're all for it if it's all right with you."

"Well, I'll have to talk to your father first," she hedged.

"But he might not be back for weeks," he pleaded, "and we need to go now while the weather is good. *Please*."

"Well..." She hesitated, frowning. She didn't like being talked into something that her instincts warned her against. "If you stay just one night."

"But it'll take us a day to get there and a day to get back. If we stay just one night, we won't have any time left to explore."

"Two nights, then, but only if—"

"Thanks! I've got to go."

"But what if—"

He was already gone, the screen door slamming before she could finish her sentence. She stood there with her mouth open, her words hanging in midair.

Will ran along the dirt road toward John's house for as long as he could. Then, out of breath, he walked the rest of the way. He ran up the back steps and opened the door as though he lived there.

"Hi, Mrs. Hamilton," he said, bounding into the kitchen.

"Good morning, Will," she answered.

"Is John here?"

"The last time I saw him, he was out on the pier, crabbing."

"Thanks!"

"Would you like something before you—" But the door had already closed behind him.

Will ran around the side of the house to the pier. As he turned the corner, a dog sleeping on the porch jumped up and barked.

"It's just me, Lady," he called as he flew past.

The old retriever wagged her tail and settled back on the porch floor.

John was sitting on the end of the wharf with his bare legs hanging over the edge. A crab net was in one hand, and a string projected down into the water from the other. Will slowed as he approached him. He watched as John slowly pulled up the string until the chicken neck and weight tied to the end were just visible in the murky water. A large crab was holding on to it with its claws while it fed on the meat.

Will stopped and watched as John eased the net down into the water, so it didn't make a ripple, then moved it toward the crab, who eyed it suspiciously. The net drew closer, and at the last second the crab released its hold on the bait and dove for the bottom. But it was too late. The net swooped out, capturing its prey. John swung it up on the dock and unceremoniously dumped the crab into a washtub with a dozen others. Will hurried over to him.

"It wasn't easy, but she finally said yes," Will said.

"Great! Now let's go ask my mother," John said, putting down the crab net.

The two boys walked side by side down the wharf, already making plans. As they approached the front porch, Lady opened one eye, then closed it again.

"Mom, can Will and I sail to the fort?" John said as they walked inside. "Mrs. Davis said it was fine with her."

"Do we really need this much food?" John asked. "We're only going to be gone for a few days."

They were in Will's kitchen, loading their supplies into baskets for the trip.

"I figured it all up by meals," Will said, "and added in an extra day just in case."

"In case of what?"

231

"In case of trouble," Will replied.

"What kind of trouble?" John asked nervously.

"Haven't you heard that it's better to be safe than sorry?"

"Sorry about what?"

"I don't know," Will said, his temper growing short. "Anything could happen."

John continued to load the baskets in silence, his mind conjuring up an endless list of possible calamities that might befall them. They had made their plans over the last two days, drawing up a list of supplies they would need and poring over maps of the bay. *Destiny* had been cleaned and scrubbed until she was gleaming. They were leaving in the morning, and John was spending the night at Will's so they could get an early start.

At dinner that evening Will's mother spent most of the time between bites warning the boys to be careful. This was to be expected, an unspoken part of the bargain for letting them go.

"And if a storm comes up," she said, "take the boat straight to land and stay there until it's over."

"Yes, ma'am," Will answered.

"Be sure to wait at least half an hour after you eat before you go in the water."

"We will."

"And when you're swimming, don't go out too far, and watch out for sharks."

"Yes, ma'am."

When the meal finally concluded, the boys

hurried upstairs to finish making plans. Will spread a large chart of the bay out on the floor, and they hunched over it, plotting the different courses they could take to the fort.

"Where do you think we should land when we get there?" John asked.

"Probably somewhere along here," he said, pointing at a spot on the map. "It's not too far from the fort, but far enough from the mouth of the bay so the current won't pull us out to sea."

"What about over here?" John said, putting his finger on the map farther away.

"Too marshy," Will replied. "Snakes and mosquitoes."

"Uhhh!" John shivered. His dislike of snakes was something Will teased him about at every opportunity.

They went over their plans until late in the night. Will was busy plotting a different course they could take, and when he looked up to ask John a question, he found his friend asleep on the floor. He covered him with a blanket, climbed into bed himself, and immediately fell asleep.

The boys were up early, and Will's mother had a big breakfast waiting for them. After eating, they finished loading the boat and cast off just as the sun was coming up. But the bay was dead calm, and they had to paddle away from the dock. An hour later the house was still plainly visible behind them. Will dozed, his arm resting against the tiller while the sail hung uselessly above them. Then the air began to stir, and the sail snapped taut. The boat picked up speed, her bow knifing through the smooth water, and they were on their way at last.

The summer breeze blew steadily, and they made good time. In the distance several ships moved along the channel, and they spent the morning trying to guess their ports of call.

"I'll bet that one's bound for Havana to pick up a load of lumber," John said.

"Not a chance! Look at how low she's riding. I think she's loaded with cotton, and headed to New York."

"Look, there's one of the bay boats," John said, pointing.

They could just make out the steam-driven side-wheeler that ferried cargo and people from the Eastern Shore to Mobile and back. Even as far away as Will lived, they could hear the whistle when they docked in Fairhope.

"Coming about!" Will called as he turned the tiller hard to port.

The boat swung around, then filled again with the wind, and they surged forward on a different tack.

"We're making good time," Will noted. "If the wind holds, we should reach the fort in plenty of time to set up camp and go exploring."

As if in answer, a gust heeled *Destiny* far over, and the boys yelled in delight.

They ate their lunch long before the sun had reached its zenith, and the land ahead of them grew steadily closer as the day wore on. The open bay had been choppy, but as they approached the narrow spit of land that formed the border between the bay and the gulf, the water grew calm.

The boys could see the Civil War fort in the distance and steered to the east of it. They were still a few hundred yards from shore when the land blocked the wind, slowing their progress to a halt. John pulled up the centerboard, and they lowered the sails, paddling the rest of the way. When the water was shallow enough, they hopped out and pulled *Destiny* the last few yards to shore. As a precaution, Will carried the anchor as far inland as the rope would allow, digging its points in the ground.

Walking across the narrow peninsula, they found a spot on the gulf as far as possible from the mosquito-infested marshes that lined much of the bay. They set up their tent and carried the food and supplies over from the boat. Then they gathered driftwood from the beach and chopped it up for firewood. Their work completed, the boys stood back and admired their new home. It was still daylight, so they decided to walk down the beach to the point where the gulf met the bay. Distant thunderheads rose high in the sky, bringing the chance of an afternoon shower.

As they walked, Will kept his eyes on the ground, looking for anything the waves might have washed up. He stopped and reached down to pick up something shiny that protruded from the sand. After washing it off in the water, he looked at the gold locket in his hand. It was missing the chain, but except for a few scratches and dents, it appeared to be in good condition.

"Let me see," John said, straining to get a look at what his friend had found.

Will dried it on his shirt and examined it carefully.

"It says 'To Walter from Marie' on one side, and 'I will love you always' on the other," he said, peering closely at the barely legible engraving.

"Open it up and see what's inside," John prodded.

Will tried to open it, but years of salt water had frozen the hinge shut. He took out his pocketknife and pried carefully between the two halves, slowly working them apart. Finally it lay open in his hand. On one side was a badly faded photograph of a young woman, while the other half still held a lock of dark hair behind the hazy glass.

"How do you think it got here?" John asked.

"I don't know." Will shrugged. "Maybe whoever was wearing it died in the war, or maybe he was stationed at the fort and lost it walking along the beach."

"Which side do you think he was on?"

Will looked at the locket and thought for a minute. "I guess there's really no way to tell," he said.

The boys stood looking at the little piece of history that lay open in Will's hand, then he closed it and put it in his pocket. They walked on to the point and stared up at the solemn walls that guarded the entrance to the bay. Across the channel they could see its sister fort in the distance.

"This is where it happened," Will said. "The largest naval battle of the Civil War. Admiral Farragut decided to brave the mines the South had put across the mouth of the bay and sail past the fire from the forts. That's when he said his famous words, 'Damn the torpedoes. Full speed ahead!'"

"I'll bet it was loud with all the cannons firing and everything," John added, looking out over the water.

"Yeah, and the smoke must have been so thick you could barely see."

They stood on the beach with only time separating them from the battle that once had raged there. They could almost feel the ghostly march of feet on the sand and see the faint outlines of ships heading into the bay. The sound of cannon fire and the acrid stench of gunpowder welled up around them as they stood transfixed.

There was a blinding flash and an almost simultaneous boom. The boys jumped as a bolt of lightning struck not far from them, and the past disappeared as the present-day storm was upon them. The smell of ozone filled the air, and they ran down the beach toward their tent as the first drops of rain started to hit around them. Another brilliant flash split the sky, and a lone pine less than a hundred feet away was splintered into kindling. The force of the blast knocked them off their feet, and they lay dazed in the sand, unable to hear over the loud ringing in their ears.

Will struggled to his feet and pulled John up. They staggered through the pouring rain to their tent and fell inside, where they lay panting, their eyes wide with fear. Outside, the storm raged and lightning illuminated the translucent walls of the tent. The canvas shuddered in the wind, the flimsy fabric seeming to offer little protection. Gradually the fury of the storm passed, and the thunder grew distant. The rain fell steadily but peacefully now as the wind died down. Soon all that was left was the sound of water dripping off the tent flaps, and for the first time the boys dared to move.

Will lit the lantern, and its yellow glow pushed the darkness back to the edges of the tent. They watched as the night tried to slip through cracks in the tent walls, pooling behind the baskets and flowing around their sleeping bags. The boys looked around nervously at the encroaching shadows, and their eyes darted back and forth as the lantern sputtered and hissed. A howl in the distance cut through the night, sending shivers up their spines. It was answered by another, closer than the first.

Outside, the boys heard something moving slowly around the tent, and they strained their ears trying to make it out. For long minutes they would hear nothing, then it would start again with the faint snap of a twig or the silent intake of a drawn breath. They dared not move as the night pressed against the frail walls, and at times it seemed that the light from the lantern was all that kept the tent from caving in around them.

After what seemed like hours, their eyes grew heavy and their heads began to nod. They dozed for minutes at a time, only to jerk awake and look around them. The blackness that had been inching its way forward under cover of sleep seemed to quickly retreat to its hiding place. Finally even the thought of their vigil left them, and they plunged headlong into sleep.

Chapter 25

The Gathering Gloom

Morning dawned bright and clear, and the storm of last night was forgotten. The boys awoke with the sun and looked out the tent flap at the new day. Breakers rolled across the bar and up onto the beach, and gulls circled a school of fish just offshore.

Will grabbed his rod and waded out to his waist in the warm water, with John right behind him. The gulf in front of them churned as fish cut through the school of bait. Leaping upward, their smooth sides glittering in the morning light, they would twist and turn in the air before falling back into the sea. Waves washed over the boys as they tried to get closer to the action.

Will was the first to cast, hurling his spoon out as far as he could and reeling it back through the school. Almost at once he had a strike, and he began backing toward shore, keeping constant pressure on the line until he stood on the beach. After pulling his catch through the shallow water onto the sand, he put his bare foot on the side of the fish as he removed the hook.

"It's a blue," he called out to John, holding it up.

John looked over at Will while he reeled in his line. Then his attention was diverted as his rod jerked violently. Soon two almost identical bluefish lay side by side in the sand. They spent the next hour fishing the school as it moved slowly along the beach. After they had caught all they could eat, they continued to cast just for the sheer joy of it, releasing the rest.

The school moved off down the beach, and John started a fire while Will cleaned the fish. Soon their pungent odor mixed with the wood smoke as the filets sizzled in the pan. Will slid the steaming pieces onto plates, and the boys dug in, breaking off chunks with their fingers. They used cornbread they had brought from home to mop up the juices, wiping their plates clean.

Full and content, they lay on the warm sand and looked out over the gulf. A sandpiper scurried along at the waterline, its feet moving faster than their eyes could see. In the distance a ship passed the fort, heading into the bay. Soon the heat of the midmorning sun forced them up, and John straightened the camp while Will washed out the dishes in the gulf. He watched as minnows darted around his legs after the bits of fish and cornbread that were floating in the water. Their chores done, they decided to spend the rest of the day exploring the old fort.

The boys walked along the beach until they neared the mouth of the bay, then headed inland through the tall grass and sea oats to the fort wall. Following it, they came to an arched brick entrance, its massive iron gates broken and twisted.

They stepped inside the tunnel that led into the fort and stopped. It was cool and dark, and coming out of the bright sun made it impossible to see anything in the gloomy interior. Water, left over from the storm the night before, dripped from the roof, forming puddles on the floor. Will took a candle stub out of his pocket and lit it, and they started forward, the sound of their footsteps echoing down the tunnel walls.

The boys moved slowly in their small circle of light. Ahead of them they could see the other end of the tunnel, overgrown with brush. The entrance behind them grew smaller, but the opening ahead didn't seem any closer. They stopped at the sound of something scurrying away in the shadows, and a draft from an unseen side passage blew out their candle.

"I hope there aren't any snakes in here," Will said as he fumbled for his matches in the dark.

"Did you say snakes?" John asked, the possibility occurring to him for the first time.

Then, without warning, Will plunged forward and disappeared. John spun around in the dark, groping blindly for him.

"Will! Where are you?" he called out.

"I'm okay, I just tripped," Will said from the floor of the tunnel. "But I dropped the candle."

They felt around the floor without success.

"It could be anywhere," John said.

"Well, we'll just have to do without it," Will told him. "Come on."

Sliding their feet across the floor to avoid stepping in another hole, they finally reached the other end and had to fight their way through the brush that blocked the opening. They emerged into the sunlight and looked around in awe at the walls of the abandoned fort surrounding them. The ground was overgrown in waist-high weeds, but they managed to force their way to the center of the compound. From there the majesty of the fort rose around them in all directions.

"Look at this place," Will said in hushed tones. "It's like an abandoned castle."

"Yeah," John added, his eyes wide. "I've never seen anything like it."

"Hey," Will said, pointing, "those steps lead up to the top of the wall."

The boys pushed through the underbrush, making their way up the crumbling brick steps to the rampart and looking back at the fort.

"Everywhere you look there are passageways and tunnels," John said, staring at other barely visible entrances. "We could spend a week exploring them all!"

"Look, there's a big hole in the wall!" Will said.

They walked over to the breached section.

"I'll bet it happened during the battle," John added, examining the broken bricks.

They sat on the parapet facing the gulf and dangled their feet over the edge. Far below them the green water beckoned. In the distance they could see their tent and the smoke from the remains of their morning fire.

"Let's look around some more," Will said. "We can start by walking all the way around the wall."

The boys hopped down and made their way around the perimeter of the fort. Weeds and bushes were growing out of cracks in the brickwork, giving the effect more of an exotic garden than a stark military facility. Will found a minié ball wedged between two bricks, and John unearthed what was left of a rusty bayonet.

While Will searched for more artifacts, John hid behind a retaining wall and began pelting him with dirt clods. Will retaliated, and soon a full-fledged war had broken out. Will took cover behind a pile of bricks while John lobbed round after round in his direction. After a few minutes of relentless bombardment, John realized that his barrage was going unanswered.

Raising his head carefully—clod at the ready—John looked over the wall. Nothing. He stood up and glanced around him suspiciously. Without warning a clod hit him square in the back, and a rain of projectiles began falling all around him. Too late he turned and saw Will standing on the wall behind him. John tried to get off a round or two but was obviously outgunned. He waved his arms to signal his surrender, and Will hopped down triumphantly.

"How did you do that?" John asked, amazed. "I had you pinned down."

"Come on, I'll show you."

The boys raced over to the pile of bricks, and Will pointed to a small opening behind it.

"It joins a larger tunnel that comes out over there," he said, pointing to an entrance behind John's former position.

"Follow me."

Will dropped down into the opening and disappeared, with John reluctantly following. John had to crawl on his hands and knees through the small tunnel until it merged with a larger passage where he could walk upright. He had lost sight of Will ahead of him, but he could see light filtering in from the surface and made his way toward it. Suddenly something grabbed him from behind and he screamed, running blindly down the tunnel to the exit.

"John, wait! It's only me," Will called after him.

John climbed the narrow brick steps at the end of the tunnel and emerged into the sunlight. He was still breathing hard from the scare when Will caught up with him.

"I had you going there, didn't I?" Will said with a smile.

"Naw, I knew it was you all along," he replied with false bravado.

"I don't know, you looked pretty scared to me," Will said, continuing to badger him.

"I was just kidding. Who else could it have been?"

As he took the gentle ribbing, John glanced over Will's shoulder at the other side of the fort, and his eyes grew wide. He tried to get Will's attention, but Will was still busy enjoying his practical joke. In desperation he spun Will around and pointed across the courtyard.

"Look!"

"What? I don't see anything," Will said, following his outstretched arm.

"Over there, in that tunnel!"

Will put up a hand to shade his eyes. "There's nothing there," he said.

"Someone was standing there, didn't you see him?" John said. "He had a beard and long hair."

"Was his name Blackbeard by any chance?"

"Will, I'm not kidding," John said, looking pale. "He had a walking stick in his hand and was staring at us."

"Well, where is he now?"

"I don't know," John said. "I guess he stepped back into the tunnel."

"Nice try," Will said, "but it won't work."

"It's not a joke, I tell you. I saw him standing there as plain as day."

Will studied John's face and could tell he was serious. "Okay, let's have a look."

"But—"

"But what?"

"He might still be there."

"Well, there's only one way to find out," Will said, starting to walk around the wall to the other side of the fort.

John hesitated for a moment, then set off after him. They walked along the wall until they reached the steps that led down to the tunnel. When they got to the bottom, Will approached the shadowy opening, but John grabbed his arm and pulled him back.

"I don't know if that's such a good idea," he whispered.

Will shook him off and started again for the opening when they heard the sound of a rock skittering across the bricks of the tunnel floor. They ducked behind a bush and waited breathlessly, then crept to the entrance and peered around the corner. Light from the other end indicated that this tunnel also went all the way through the fort wall.

"I don't see anyone," Will said. "Maybe it was just a brick falling out of the ceiling."

John looked down at the ground in front of them and pointed to a set of footprints clearly imbedded in the soft sand. They looked at each other.

"What should we do now?" John asked.

"Follow them, I guess."

"But what if he's hiding in the tunnel somewhere?"

Will thought for a minute. "Let's go back up on the wall and see what's on the other side," he suggested.

They retraced their steps and soon were back on top of the fort wall. After crawling to the low parapet, they looked over the edge. The entrance below appeared deserted. Will noticed a pine tree that had grown right up against the wall and walked over to it, motioning for John to follow.

"We can climb down here," he said, indicating the tree.

Will grabbed the trunk and hoisted himself over the wall, disappearing from sight. The tree swayed violently as he made his way down, then the movement stopped. John looked over the side to see him standing at the foot of the wall below.

"Come on!" Will said.

John eased himself over the edge, copying Will's descent, and together they made their way to the fort entrance. The gate was permanently wedged open by windblown sand, and a set of footprints was clearly visible in it, leading away from the fort down a narrow trail.

The boys followed the trail through the woods as it led north toward the open bay. The footprints would vanish where pine needles covered the path but always reappeared in the next patch of loose sand.

Abruptly the underbrush ended and they were standing on the shore of the bay not far from the spot where they had tied up their boat. The tracks followed the shoreline, heading away from the mouth of the bay. But as far as they could see, the narrow shore appeared deserted. The boys soon came upon *Destiny,* still tied securely. The tracks stopped, circled around the boat, then continued on along the shore.

"What should we do now?" John asked.

"Follow them and see where they lead."

"But he left us alone, so maybe we should leave him alone."

"We're not doing anything wrong," Will said. "We're just out for an afternoon stroll."

"I don't know..." John said, hesitating.

"We've come this far, let's see who he is and why he's here," Will urged.

"Okay, but I don't like it."

They set out once again, the footprints drawing them on. Half a mile down the shore, the tracks turned inland on a narrow path. Ahead they saw a curl of smoke issuing from a pine thicket.

The trail emerged into a clearing in the woods. In the middle stood a small cabin raised high off the ground, with four living pine trees acting as corner posts. Rough board-and-batten walls ended in a gabled roof, and a stovepipe protruding through it emitted the smoke they had seen before. Crude steps—

hewed from driftwood—led up to a salvaged ship hatch that served as a door. The boys crouched behind a clump of palmettos and waited, looking for any signs of life inside.

"I don't think he's home," Will whispered after they had been there for several minutes. "Let's take a look around."

"No," John said firmly. "We've seen enough."

"But we still don't know who lives here or why," he countered.

"We don't need to know."

"Come on, where's your sense of adventure?" Will said.

"I think I left it back at the fort," John replied. "Now, let's go back to camp."

Will ignored him and ran across the clearing to the house. He scanned the area and signaled for John to follow him. From the safety of the woods, John shook his head and refused to budge.

Giving the clearing one more look, Will started up the steps. Halfway to the top, there was a loud creak as he put his weight on a step. He froze, his heart in his throat. When nothing happened, he quickly took the remaining steps up to the landing. Peering in the window, he cupped his hands around his face to keep out the glare, then slowly pushed open the door and slipped inside.

John crouched nervously in the bushes, uncertain what to do next. If Will was caught, the nearest help was a day's sail away. The seconds ticked by as he waited. He had almost given up when Will reappeared in the doorway and waved him over. John shook his head, and Will gestured with more urgency.

"There's no one here," he called softly.

John looked around and against his better judgment ran across the clearing and up the steps.

"You've got to see this!" Will said excitedly.

"We really ought to get out of here," John said. "He could come back any minute."

"You can't leave until you go inside," Will told him.

"You can tell me about it later. Now let's go."

"*No!* It's important," Will said, steering John toward the door and guiding him inside.

Will closed it behind them and watched John's mouth drop open as he saw the interior of the cabin. It was a small room with a few plain pieces of furniture. But what caused John's eyes to grow wide was not what was in the room, but what was on it.

The entire room had been transformed into one continuous mural. The ceiling was painted sky blue and dotted with clouds. On the eastern side, a sunrise had been painted, the glow of the new day peeking out to illuminate the world. On the opposite wall, a sunset shot streaks of gold across the sky. Against this celestial backdrop, the undersides of pelicans and seagulls soared across the ceiling on the wind. Below them, each of the four walls was painted to display a different local scene.

The north wall depicted the bay coastline, with crabs scurrying along the shore and a blue heron hunting in the shallow water for fish. A mullet was frozen forever in midleap, and a skunk peeked out of the tall grass that lined the shore.

The south wall showed the gulf beach in all its brilliance. Sea oats spread out over dunes, and sandpipers ran along the water's edge. Ghost crabs were half-hidden in their holes, their eyestalks watching for the first sign of danger, and a sea turtle pushed slowly up the beach, searching for a spot to lay her eggs.

To the east was marshland, where a cottonmouth moccasin glided effortlessly through the black water. A red-winged blackbird tilted sideways as it perched on a cattail stalk, and an alligator sunned itself—its red eyes staring out hatefully at the world.

The final wall was a coastal forest, its tall pines reaching for the sky. A woodpecker looked out from a hole in the top of a dead tree, while a black bear was doing its best to relieve a swarm of angry bees of its winter supply of honey. On the ground, a raccoon was sitting on its hind legs, eating a fish under a spread of palmetto leaves.

Even the floor had not escaped the artist's eye. The green water of the gulf crashed against the beach wall, mingling in the center of the room with the muddy water of the bay. Fish could be seen breaking the surface, and spray blew from the blowhole of a dolphin. Near one corner, the fin of a hammerhead shark cut through the water, sending a chill up John's spine.

"Will, what *is* all this?" he asked.

"I don't know," Will said, shaking his head.

"But who would live way out here, anyway?"

"Maybe someone who couldn't quite fit in anywhere," Will said thoughtfully. "There's something else, though. Look over here."

He led John over to the corner of the room where the beach met the forest. Fresh gray paint obscured the painting, beginning to cover the beautiful scenes on each side. John reached out and touched it, pulling back dark-stained fingers.

"What does it mean?" he asked, confused.

"I'm not sure," Will said, "but I have a feeling we should sail home as soon as we can."

They backed out of the cabin slowly—taking in the room one last time—then ran down the steps and across the clearing, disappearing back up the trail.

After they had gone, silence returned to the clearing, broken only by the sound of the wind whispering in the trees. A minute passed, then two, and a man appeared from the edge of the forest where a moment before there had been no one. The afternoon light gave the impression that he had materialized from the trees themselves. He looked for a long time down the path the boys had taken. Then he turned and walked slowly across the clearing and up the steps to the cabin, closing the door behind him.

Picking up a wide brush and his palette from the table, he studied the wall before him intently. Of all the multicolored hues at his command, he chose to dip his brush in white, then mix it with black to form a swirl of gray. He lifted the laden brush and paused, sorrow filling his eyes as he stared at the walls before him. Then, starting where he had left off, he began to paint with large, sweeping strokes— slowly at first, and then ever faster, his eyes blazing with a dark intensity.

Outside, the wind changed from a whisper to a low moan in the gathering gloom.

Chapter 26

The Storm

Will and John ran the whole way back to the boat, then turned south to their camp on the beach. Collapsing in the tent, they lay panting on their sleeping bags. After he had gotten his breath back, Will sat up and opened the tent flap.

"It's too late to start back now," he said, looking at the darkening sky. "We'll have to stay here tonight and leave first thing in the morning."

"But what about the hermit? He's bound to know where we are," John said, worried.

"I don't think he'll bother us," Will replied. "I'll bet he knew we were here all along."

Still, he sat in the opening and kept watch until night rolled in.

They woke up to the sound of rain pelting the tent in the gray morning light. The wind had picked up, and waves pounded the beach. Will didn't like the look of the low, fast-moving clouds that obscured the sky, but the rain stopped and they decided to make a run for it before the storm got any worse.

They broke camp quickly and carried everything over to the boat. The tide had risen during the night, and *Destiny* was no longer beached securely but floated freely in the shallow water, held only by the anchor Will had set when they arrived. They stowed their gear and pushed the little boat away from the shore.

Near land the water was still calm, but as they got farther out, whitecaps began to form and the bay grew rough. Will decided on the shortest route home, even though it would take them far from the safety of shore. The following sea would not be as rough as if they were going into it, and with the weather deteriorating, there was no time to lose.

Their relaxing, sunny sail of two days before was forgotten and replaced by a white-knuckled roller-coaster ride. The sail strained at the riggings, and the bow dug deeper and deeper into the waves. A cold rain fell steadily now, stinging their skin. The boys put on their slickers and huddled low in the bottom of the boat as the wind intensified. Water broke over the bow each time they plowed through a big swell, and the farther they got from the protection of the shore, the rougher the bay became. The wind now had a moaning quality that Will had not heard before, and he was forced to admit that this was no ordinary storm.

"We're taking on too much water!" he yelled to John. "Get the bucket and start bailing!"

John nodded and moved one of the sections of slatted flooring to give him room to work. Six inches of water sloshed around in the bottom of the boat, and it was getting deeper all the time. He found a bucket and began scooping up the water and dumping it over the side, trying to keep ahead of the storm.

Will's eyes were fixed on the horizon when he noticed a small tear starting in the corner of the mainsail where the boom and mast met. He watched as it spread slowly across the taut canvas. He tapped John on the back and pointed to the sail.

"See if you can stop it from getting any worse," he said. "The repair kit is under the bow."

John crawled forward, found the sewing kit, and, balancing precariously, made a cross-stitch in front of the advancing tear. It continued to inch forward until it reached the reinforced cloth, then stopped. He tried to mend the split with needle and thread, but the sail was stretched so tightly that it was impossible to pull the two halves together. The best he could do was take some of the strain off by sewing a spiderweb of thread back and forth across the opening. This task accomplished, he returned to bailing, trying to make up for lost time.

The sky didn't lighten as the morning passed but seemed to grow darker instead. The bay was so rough now that going over the waves slowed the boat down, keeping the boys from making as good time as they would have. They hadn't raised the jib at all and had reefed in the mainsail as much as possible, but there was still too much canvas for the strong wind. Often the shore was invisible behind the clouds and rain, and Will had to navigate by dead reckoning, using only the compass mounted near the tiller.

By early afternoon the rain had slacked up and the clouds had lifted a little. Will saw land ahead and recognized the point not far from his house. Soon he could see the wharf jutting out into the bay and headed for it. The waves were too high to try to dock at the pier, so he turned the boat straight for land. As they neared the shore, he saw the waves crashing fiercely and steered for the beach, helped along by a big breaker.

"John! Raise the centerboard!" he yelled.

John pulled it up just as the bay disappeared beneath them and was replaced by dry land. The water was so high that they were deposited on what had previously been the lawn. A dim figure appeared out of the rain, and Will's father grabbed the bowline, holding the boat fast before the next wave could take them back out again.

Hurrying, they lowered the sail and unstepped the mast, then together they turned *Destiny* over on her side and drained out the water. Their load lightened, they dragged the boat across the yard and into the storage shed. The wind was a steady howl now, and Will's father motioned them toward the house. As they ran across the yard, a strong gust knocked Will and John down. Mr. Davis helped them to their feet and hustled them up the front steps onto the porch.

Will's mother, who had been watching for them out the window all day, opened the front door. The knob was ripped out of her hands by the force of the wind, throwing the door against the wall. They staggered inside, and Mr. Davis had to put all his strength behind the door to close it.

His mother grabbed Will and hugged him so hard that he could barely breathe, then pushed him back to arm's length.

"I was so worried! What do you mean going out in a storm like this?" she scolded, near tears.

"It wasn't this bad when we started," Will said, "and we wanted to get home as soon as we could."

"It was a foolish thing to do," she said. "You could have drowned." But her eyes had already softened, and she hugged him again.

Even with the shutters bolted and the doors tightly locked, the storm could still be felt. The house rocked under the strain, and years of accumulated dust blew up from between the floorboards. The wind was a constant presence now, its pitch changing from a low moan to a shrieking howl as each gust hit the house.

"I need to go home and let my folks know that I'm okay," John said.

Mr. Davis shook his head. "I'm afraid you won't be going anywhere for a while," he told him, looking out the window.

"Get out of those wet things before you catch your death of cold," Will's mother instructed all of them.

"Catching cold may be the least of our problems," Mr. Davis replied grimly, pulling off his shirt.

Will's mother went in the kitchen to fix them something to eat. When they had dressed, she served up bowls of steaming soup and cornbread. The boys were starved, and it wasn't until they were halfway through eating that they managed to tell their story. When they talked about the hermit, Will's mother and father glanced at each other. There had been rumors that someone was living on the beach near the old fort, but until now that was all they had been. The boys reached the end of their tale, and Will looked over at his father.

"I thought you were going to be gone awhile?" he said.

"I finished up my business early and decided to come home. When I got to Mobile there was talk of a big storm coming, so I took the last bay boat that was going to try to make the run."

He was interrupted by a loud crash from the

backyard as the wind toppled one of the big oaks. They looked at one another, a trace of fear showing for the first time on every face.

"This is going to be a big one, I can feel it," Mr. Davis said.

By the time they finished eating, it was the middle of the afternoon, but outside it was perpetual twilight. The boys peered through cracks in the shuttered windows at the bay. The wind was blowing toward the house from across the water, and the front yard was covered in windblown foam.

"It looks like a root beer at the drugstore," John said, turning to Will with his eyes wide.

"Yeah, I had no idea it could get this rough."

The wharf was taking quite a beating. The tide was still rising, and the water was almost level with the deck. Waves crashed over it constantly, sending spray high in the air. As they watched, boards were wrenched free and thrown up on the ever encroaching shore.

The wind was unrelenting. It was a thing alive, tearing at the very fabric of the world. As they watched, they could almost feel the nails that held the tin on the wharf roof loosening from the constant pull. A small corner of the tin would start to flap until half the sheet was vibrating violently. Then, as if sensing its weakness, a violent gust would rip the sheet from its mooring and send it tumbling through the air high over the house.

The water continued to advance up the hill, and they began to wonder if the land could contain it. As the sky grew darker, the sound of limbs crashing and trees uprooting became commonplace occurrences. The house shook violently as something rumbled past not far from them. The bay had now reached the front steps, and waves began to slosh over the porch and seep under the door. A shutter upstairs was ripped from its hinges, and they heard the sound of breaking glass, followed by a change in air pressure that caused their ears to pop.

"Boys, come with me!" Mr. Davis yelled above the storm.

He grabbed a hammer and nails and ran up the stairs. The upstairs bedroom was in chaos, the wind's wrath pouring through the chink in the house's armor. Mr. Davis lifted the hall door off its hinges and tried to cover the broken window with it, but the force of the wind was too great, knocking him to the floor. He struggled to his feet, and the boys helped him pick it up for another attempt.

"Wait until there's a lull!" he told them.

For what seemed like ages, the wind refused to slacken, then it paused momentarily to catch its breath.

"Now!" he yelled.

They shoved the door against the open window, pushing with all their might to hold it there. Mr. Davis drove nail after nail through it into the window facing until his arms ached. The wind gathered its strength and rushed at the house again, but the nails held. Furious, the storm rained blow after blow against it. Clapboard was peeled from the outside walls, roofing was ripped from the rafters, bricks were hurled from the chimney, but the house held firm against the onslaught.

They returned downstairs to find Will's mother stuffing towels under the door in a vain attempt to keep out the rising water. Mr. Davis and the boys grabbed mops and towels, wringing the water into buckets. At first it appeared they were winning, but the water kept coming. It continued to rise, and there was little they could do but watch as it inched slowly but steadily upward. Soon it began to seep between the cracks in the floorboards as the crawl space under the house filled up.

They gave up trying to stop the water and concentrated on moving things out of its path. Will's father and the boys carried all the furniture they could upstairs, while his mother removed papers and books from the secretary. The small upstairs was quickly growing crowded, so Will's father drove nails as high as he could in the walls downstairs and hung the chairs from them. By now the tide was knee deep in the house and still rising. Will's father turned out all the kerosene lamps except one, which he held in his hand.

"Everyone upstairs, we've done all we can down here," he said, herding them up the stairs.

"But my things! We haven't gotten all my silver or plates yet," Will's mother pleaded.

"There's no time," he said. "They'll have to stay in the cabinets."

Upstairs, water dripped everywhere through

the leaking roof and poured in where it was missing completely. It was now pitch black outside, and the storm showed no signs of abating. A gust of wind through the open roof blew out the lamp, and darkness descended to cover them completely. Their eyes were now useless, and the sounds of the storm filled their thoughts. They huddled together for warmth and security in a corner of Will's bedroom, while the house shook violently as floating trees and pilings slammed against it.

Then, without any warning, the wind stopped. One minute all was fury and violence, the next it was quiet and still. They didn't move, afraid even to breathe.

"It's stopped," Will said.

They stood up cautiously and looked through the gaping hole in the roof. Above them the stars shone brightly in a clear sky, and a flock of seagulls circled overhead. Without the power of the wind to drive them, the waves in the bay quickly died down.

Will's father lit the lamp, and they made their way downstairs. The knee-deep water was littered with their belongings, and Mrs. Davis looked around at the mess in dismay. They forced open the front door and walked out onto the caved-in porch. The moon was shining on the bay—its light reflecting off the water. There was nothing to be seen of the wharf under the high tide, and they could hear *Destiny* bumping against the walls of the shed as she floated in her once dry berth.

"How could it just stop like that?" Will asked.

Across the bay, the moon slipped behind a cloud, and they felt the wind begin to stir.

"I've always heard that it's calm at the center of a storm," Mr. Davis said. "This isn't over yet. Everyone back in the house."

He pushed them all inside and bolted the door behind them.

The wind hit hard from the opposite direction, and the house bent once more before the storm. They waded through the main room and back up the stairs to huddle again in a corner. But while the wind was almost as strong as before, it now blew from the land rather than off the water. There were no pounding waves, and the bay was pushed away from the house. Soon the water had retreated and the hill was once again visible.

The hurricane raged on through the night, gradually losing its power as it moved inland. When dawn broke, only the tattered remnants of clouds marred the blue sky. The inside of the house was in shambles, and foul-smelling mud from the bottom of the bay covered everything.

Mr. Davis opened the front door, and they emerged into the light. The porch had collapsed, and they had to thread their way carefully through the broken rafters and splintered boards to make their way outside. The world around them was turned upside down. Trees had been uprooted and broken like matchsticks, debris covered the yard, and a few twisted pilings were all that was left of the wharf. They wandered forward aimlessly, trying to absorb the devastation around them.

They turned and stared up at the house, seeing the total power of the storm. Half the roof was gone, and sections of siding had been ripped away, exposing the sturdy framework underneath. Pilings had been used as battering rams, leaving neatly punched holes in the downstairs walls. Shutters were missing and windows smashed. Several trees lay across the house, causing it to twist and bow under their weight.

For a long time no one moved as they stood there, overcome by the sight. Finally John broke the spell, dashing off down the road to check on his family. Will's father forced open the door to the toolshed and returned with an ax, its oiled blade shining in the sun. He walked to the side of the house, stood still for a moment, then raised it high over his head and brought it down hard.

The quiet of the day was broken by the ringing thud as the ax found its mark. The blade wedged deep into the trunk of an oak that had fallen against the side of the house, and he levered the handle back and forth to work it loose. Again he raised the blade high and again it fell, each stroke driving a wedge between the anarchy that surrounded them. Over and over the ax fell, its rhythm acting as a cadence to build their shattered lives around.

It was late by the time the old man's story ended. The light from a single yellow bulb illuminated the wharf, casting everything else into shadow. Josh stopped writing and looked over at Mr. Davis.

"You were lucky to survive," he said.

"Others were not so fortunate," the old man replied.

"What happened to the hermit?" he asked.

"A few days later my father took us back to look for him, but the whole area had been swept clean by the storm," he said. "There wasn't a tree left standing, nothing but flat sand as far as the eye could see. He was never heard from again. The fort survived, of course, and now it's a historic landmark. Have you ever been there?"

"Once, when I was little," Josh said. "But I think I'd like to see it again."

"You might be disappointed; it won't be like I remembered it. The grounds are well kept, and tourists are constantly milling around."

"I'd like to see it anyway," he said, closing his notebook. "I'll use my imagination."

Mr. Davis got up and walked over to the railing, leaning his elbows on it, and Josh joined him. They stood there, staring up into the night sky.

"You'll find as you grow older and look back, Josh, that there are certain moments in your life that stand out as brightly as stars on a moonless night. They're not always the ones you expect, either," he said, turning and looking at the boy. "Sometimes, like the hurricane, you'll recognize them when they're happening. But often it's the little things that you weren't even aware of at the time that fill your thoughts. I've tried to share some of my memories with you, but there are many more that I'll never be able to express."

A shooting star streaked across the heavens, briefly lighting up the dark sky.

"Did you see it?" Mr. Davis asked.

Josh nodded.

"They only last a second, but for that moment they're the brightest thing in the sky," he said, looking over at the boy. "We're like that, too. Here for just a fleeting instant and then gone."

Chapter 27

Red Sky at Night

The afternoon sun reflected off the water, and a warm breeze blew toward land. The screen door opened, and Mr. Davis walked onto the porch. He closed the door quietly behind him, unwilling to break the spell that the day cast. Thrusting his hands deep in his pockets, he turned to face the bay. His eyes never grew tired of the sight, and there were times when he felt it was all that kept him going.

He walked slowly onto the wharf and looked down at the weathered planks that he and his father had replaced so long ago.

"We grew up together, you and I," he said to them, "and now we've grown old together, too."

Over the years the boards had become rough, but they had been worn smooth again by the passing of many feet. The two halves blended together to form something more than each one alone. When everything goes right, he thought, it forms something beautiful. For what is nature without the eyes of man to admire her?

He watched an ant crossing the board at his feet. It approached a crack as if it were a wide ravine, and a knothole in its path became the Grand Canyon. The marvel of life in all its myriad facets flashed before him. We see things through our eyes only, he thought. I see this bay spread before me like a painting, and I color it with all that it has meant to me. As if in answer, a gust of wind ruffled his white hair.

I've had a good life, he reflected, and I have no regrets. And through it all, as constant as a rock and as changeable as the weather, this bay has been here to greet me when I return. Scientists can tell you everything about it— how it was formed, the plants and animals that live in it—but they can never qualify its beauty.

He looked at the light glistening off the water and breathed in the smell of the distant sea on the breeze. Closing his eyes, he could hear the splash of a mullet as it landed in the twilight and the irregular slap of waves against the shore. This is a very special place, he knew, a holy place.

He reached the end of the wharf and could go no farther. Sitting in his old familiar chair, he rubbed his hands absently over the chair's arms. He knew this place, knew it better than anywhere else. He turned to look at the wharf behind him. Ever since he could remember, he had raced down it. Now he shuffled down it instead, but the feeling was the same. In his mind he was still twelve years old, and he could hear his boyhood friend calling him as if it were yesterday. The memories came faster and thicker until a flood of emotion poured out of him, spilling down his lined cheeks to fall drop by drop through the floor-boards into the water below.

"'When an old man dies, a library is burned to the ground,'" he muttered.

He looked down at the wrinkled hands that lay on the arms of the chair and saw them as they were in his youth. These same hands had held the rod as he fought the tarpon, had tenderly caressed his wife and picked up his newborn son, and they had reached out to Josh when he'd needed a hand on his shoulder.

He took the gold locket out of his pocket and rubbed his fingers over the names engraved on it. How did their lives turn out? he wondered. Life is a mystery, he thought, and so it should always remain.

He turned his gaze outward to the bay and watched the light dancing on the water. The sun dipped behind a cloud, and vivid reds and yellows lit up the sky. With the intervention of the clouds, he could look directly at the sun, and he watched as it slowly dropped below the horizon.

"Red sky at night, sailor's delight," he said aloud, with only the bay there to hear him.

He put his hand on his chest and could feel the beating of his heart. What is the sound of one heart beating? he mused. *All that you see before you,* came back the answer from deep within.

He felt spent, his body worn out. He closed his eyes and rested, gathering his waning strength. It would be easy to slip away like a child's balloon and drift toward the setting sun, parting the thin veil between life and death.

He opened his eyes again and noticed a speck of white on the horizon far out on the bay. As he watched it grew larger, until he could see the familiar triangular shape of a sail.

"It would be a good day for a sail," he said to himself.

A thin mist crept up from the surface of the bay to cover the water. As the boat grew closer, he squinted, trying to make her out. The fog grew thicker, and he shivered involuntarily. Then he knew who she was, and a smile played across his lips. Of course, why couldn't he see it before? It was *Destiny,* and she was here to take him home.

He relaxed his grip on the locket, and it

slipped from his fingers. It bounced once on the deck, then disappeared between a gap in the boards, hitting the water with a soft plop. Overhead, gulls circled and cried, while beyond the wharf a mullet jumped in the fading afternoon light. Waves slapped against the shore, and the bay held him close in her arms.

Chapter 28

The Sound of a Single Heartbeat

You only are immortal, the creator and maker of mankind; and we are mortal, formed of the earth, and to earth shall we return. For so did you ordain when you created me, saying, "You are dust, and to dust you shall return." All of us go down to the dust; yet even at the grave we make our song.'"

Josh opened his eyes and raised his head after the prayer was over. He stood at the end of the wharf with his mother and a dozen other friends of Mr. Davis's, including his son.

Father O'Ferrall put the prayer book on the table in front of him and looked up at them.

"Men like William Davis don't come along very often," he said, "and I've had the privilege of getting to know him these last few years.

He was a very private person, mostly keeping to himself here on the shore of this bay, but he always had words of wisdom for those whose lives he touched." He paused, took a deep breath, then continued. "The world may not note his passing, but he will be greatly missed by those of us who knew him. He has prepared a letter that he asked me to read at this time."

He picked up a sheet of paper from the table.

"'To my friends gathered here today,

"'I do not know if there is anything after death, but that isn't really my concern. What matters most is that we do the best we can with what we have been given while we are here. To live each day as if it were our last, for it may well be.

"'I've had a full life, so don't mourn my passing. Instead, take this time to look at the beauty around you. If there is a God, this bay is his most magnificent work. And every time you look at it, think of me, for it captured my heart long ago, and after today we will be one at last.'"

Father O'Ferrall put the letter back on the table and picked up a wooden box next to it.

"And now, as William has requested, we commend his ashes to the water that he held so dear."

He turned to face the bay, opened the lid, and sprinkled the ashes over the side of the wharf.

"Water is life and life is water, there cannot

be one without the other. Take your servant William into the mystery of your depths and let him remain there with you forever."

He put the empty box back on the table.

Josh stood around awkwardly after the service, unsure what to do next. Iced tea and lemonade were served, and they sat and talked at the end of the wharf, recalling things the old man had said or done. Just as the sun was being swallowed by the bay and the sky was in its full glory, a flock of pelicans glided by, their wing tips almost skimming the water. Suddenly and inexplicably, one of the great birds veered straight up, flapping its mighty wings as it rose high into the sky. They watched as its shape grew smaller and smaller, until it finally vanished from sight altogether in the gathering twilight.

The guests began to leave, and Josh and his mother stopped to offer their condolences to Mr. Davis's son on their way out. Josh could see something of the old man in him, particularly in his eyes.

"Josh, can you stop by the house tomorrow afternoon?" he asked. "I have something I would like to talk to you about."

"Sure," Josh replied. "I'll come over after my deliveries, around five."

"That'll be fine," he said. "I'll look for you then."

They turned to go. "Oh, and Josh. Thank you for coming today," he added. "It seems you meant a lot to my father these last few months."

"He meant a lot to me, too," Josh said, his eyes lowered.

They made their way across the yard and drove home in silence.

Josh closed the door to his room and took off his coat and tie. He opened the birdcage and rubbed his finger across the bird's chest.

"You remember him, don't you?" he said. The bird cocked his head at the sound of the boy's voice. "He's the one who fixed your wing."

Closing the cage, Josh looked around his room and tried to draw comfort from it. He stared at each of the photographs stuck in the frame of the mirror, including the one his mother had taken of him with Mr. Davis at graduation. Then he looked at his own face reflected in the glass and almost didn't recognize it.

He sat on the edge of the bed with his head resting in his hands, remembering. Soon the tears he had been holding back began to fall on the carpet between his feet. Tonight the bay has taken my friend, he thought, and I'll never have another like him.

Josh was a little late pulling up the drive the next afternoon. All of the people on his route had kept him a few minutes extra today to talk about Mr. Davis. Even Mrs. Bennett had said how sorry she was. Mrs. Howard had rambled on for fifteen minutes about how Mr. Davis would come over and fix things for her and how she didn't know what she would do without him. He had answered each of their personal eulogies politely, but his thoughts were elsewhere.

He stopped the car halfway up the drive and cut the engine. Looking at the cage sitting on the passenger seat next to him, Josh watched the little bird hop nervously back and forth on its perch. He picked up the cage and got out of the car, then set the cage down in the middle of the driveway. Holding open the door, he reached inside and removed the squirming bird.

"It's all right," he said in a soothing voice as he pulled the loose end of the string and carefully unwrapped the splint from around the bird's wing. "You're going to be just fine."

Josh smoothed out the feathers and held the bird for a minute, unwilling to let go. Then he slowly opened his hand, and in an instant it was gone. He watched it light on a limb not far away, where it sat preening its feathers. The bird glanced down at him and chirped loudly, then, in a flash of blue, it flew across the yard and disappeared into the trees.

Josh put the cage back in the car and drove the rest of the way down the drive. He parked and instinctively flipped up the seat and reached inside. The backseat was empty, and for the first time it hit him that all his deliveries had been made. He stepped back and eyed the seat critically, then got out the birdcage and closed the car door.

As he walked slowly to the house, Josh stopped once to look up into the branches of the trees that towered above him. The limbs swayed in the afternoon breeze, and the Spanish moss billowed like sails in the wind. He walked up the back steps and knocked on the door. It opened, and Mr. Davis's son stood in the doorway.

"Come in," he said, moving aside to let him through.

"I'm returning this," Josh said, handing him the birdcage.

"Oh?" he asked.

"I borrowed it from Mr. Davis," Josh said, "but I don't need it anymore." He put the cage on the kitchen floor.

"Have a seat, Josh," he said, indicating the chair across from him. The table was covered with papers, and he picked up a sheet in front of him and read it before continuing.

"I've been going through my father's things and found something that pertained to you."

"To me?" Josh said with a puzzled look.

"Apparently he was working on it the day he died," he said, putting down the paper and looking at the boy. "It seems that he cared a lot about you, Josh. You should take that as quite a compliment; my father wasn't the easiest person to get to know. I also found this with your name on it." He handed Josh a manila envelope.

"I'm going out on the wharf while you take a look at that," he said. "Come join me when you're through."

He slid his chair back from the table and left. Josh stared down at the envelope with his name written on the front in Mr. Davis's shaky hand. He picked it up and turned it over, almost afraid to look inside, then opened the clasp and slid the contents onto the table. It contained a small clothbound book and a single sheet of stationery. He picked up the letter first, written in the same characteristic script.

Dear Josh,

I know that if you're reading this, it means that I'm no longer with you. I imagine by now you've said your farewells, so don't dwell on it. I've had a good life and that's all anyone can ask for.

You've turned these last few months around for me, Josh, and for that I'm grateful. I thought that I had accomplished all I was supposed to, but I was wrong. You brought purpose back to my life and made me feel young again. By helping to write my stories, you made it possible for me to share them with you. I think we both learned something from it, something important.

Most people are content with just the daily affairs of life, but you and I are different. We've been given a gift that is rare in this world, the gift of understanding, of seeing deep into the heart of things. I've tried to nurture it in you and help it to grow.

Learn to use your gift, Josh, to question and see things that no one else but you can, then write about what you have learned. For only in giving back will you find fulfillment.

To further that end, I am setting up a scholarship for you to attend Spring Hill College next fall. Think of this as a parting gift, if you like. You can learn much there. Then, when you are ready, perhaps you can tell the stories that are in your heart.

I am also leaving you Destiny. You can keep her here. She is still as solid as the day she was built, but you'll have to keep her sails and ropes dry.

I wish you the best as you travel on your journey through life.

Your Friend,
William Davis

Josh read the letter through a second time, then put it back in the envelope. He picked up the book and ran his fingers over the cover. It was the copy of *The Old Man and the Sea* that Mr. Davis had loaned him the first time they had talked. Opening it, he saw an inscription on the title page:

To Josh,

All the vast beauty of the world can be found in the sound of a single heartbeat, if you take the time to listen.

William Davis.

Josh looked around the room one last time, then slipped the book and letter back into the envelope and got up from the table.

He went out to the car and opened the

door. As he was putting the envelope on the passenger seat, he noticed the notebook sitting there and picked it up. Holding it open, he looked at the pages covered with the old man's life.

Josh could see Mr. Davis's son standing at the end of the wharf, leaning against the railing, and he walked down the worn path to join him. His feet rang hollowly on the planks, and when he reached the end he stopped and stood beside him. Neither one of them said anything for a minute. Finally the old man's son spoke up.

"I intend to honor my father's wishes," he said. "I've already called the school to confirm the arrangements."

"I don't know what to say," Josh said.

The man looked at him and smiled. "You don't have to say anything, it's the way he wanted it," he said.

He looked back at the house. "This place has been in my family always, and I plan to keep it that way. I'll come here every summer for a few weeks, but the rest of the time it will be empty." He took a key out of his pocket. "I've made this for you in case you ever want to come here," he said, giving it to Josh.

"I've got something for you, too," Josh said, holding out the notebook.

"What's this?" he asked, flipping through it.

"It's something your father was working on," Josh said. "I think he would have wanted you to have it."

Mr. Davis's son closed the notebook and leaned against the railing again, his eyes sweeping the horizon. "I'm afraid that I wasn't always the son I should have been," he confessed.

"You meant a lot to him," Josh said. "He talked about it just a few days ago."

He glanced over at the boy, then turned to look back out over the bay.

Josh saw ripples approaching them across the water. "It looks like good sailing weather," he said, long before the gust of wind reached them.

Chapter 29

Full Circle

The seasons passed, summers and winters rolling by the empty windows of the house on the bay. The wharf had seen more storms, and several of the planks were missing or loose. A piece of tin flapped back and forth in the breeze while a lone pelican roosted on the peak of the wharf roof, keeping one eye peeled for fish. The bird raised its long neck at the unfamiliar sound of a car in the drive but remained where it was: watching...waiting.

A young man got out of the car and stopped to look around him, running his hand through his short blond hair. The yard had lost the manicured look it once had, but other than that everything was still the same. He opened the trunk and took out a suitcase, then carried it up the back steps and unlocked the door with his key.

Leaving the suitcase in the kitchen, he walked to the den and slowly pushed open the door. As his eyes adjusted to the dim light, he saw the worn recliner facing the fireplace, and a wave of emotion swept over him. He breathed in deeply and closed his eyes, his outstretched hand resting on the bookcase by the door to steady him.

He closed the door again and walked slowly through each room of the house, stopping at a butterfly collection mounted behind glass on the wall in the hall and a birdcage sitting on the floor in a corner. Last of all, he opened the door to the old man's bedroom and stood looking at the four-poster bed. He went over to the table next to it and examined it closely. The cherry was dark with age and there was a crack in the top, but the drawer still slid out smoothly.

He retraced his steps to the kitchen, picked up his suitcase, and carried it to the guest bedroom. After closing the back door behind him, he walked around the house to the storage shed. He opened the doors and pulled back the tarpaulin that covered the small boat. Dust motes shimmered in the sunlight as his eyes followed the gracefully curved lines of the boat and the name painted in a child's hand on the transom.

Leaving the shed, he went over to his car and took a spiral notebook off the front seat, then walked down the overgrown path to the wharf. Annoyed at the intrusion, the great bird spread its wings and dropped into a glide off the roof, letting loose a steam of pelican profanity as it slowly flapped away. He paused to watch its flight, then continued out onto the pier. Halfway down its length, he stopped at a weathered plank and crouched next to it. He reached out and touched it with his hand, then stood and walked on to the covered deck at the end.

He looked at the old chair, still there after all this time. Dropping his notebook on the deck beside it, he sat down carefully, resting his hands on the arms. Without the old man's touch, the arms had grown coarse and rough. He sat that way for a long time, looking out over the water. The bay was as beautiful as ever, and he rubbed his hands lightly on the arms of the chair as the sun sank lower until it touched the water.

He picked up the notebook beside him and opened it to the first blank page. Then, looking around him one last time, he took out a pen and began to write in a left-handed scrawl:

The beat-up old Volkswagen, radio blaring, puttered up the long drive to the house. Ancient live oaks lined the drive and formed a living arch over it. The house sat far off the road, and it wasn't until rounding the last bend that the bay came into view.